COMMENTS ON THE FIRST EDITION OF THIS VOLUME

"Sir, I have enjoyed each and every story you have published from the Dispatch Box. They are some of the best Holmes pastiches ever written, current book included. You have hinted at more stories should you be fortunate enough to discover them. I sincerely hope the Dispatch Box has a false bottom with some more adventures."

"Mr Ashton has an uncanny knack of writing stories which would fit seamlessly into the original Conan Doyle accounts. He has picked up the cadences and language use which make them hard to distinguish from the originals. This outing is no different."

"Sherlock Holmes stories are probably the most common pastiches there are. Some are decent, some are awful...

And some have the sense of somehow having been written by Conan Doyle himself. These are that last category: Doyle-esque in every sense.

You are in London near the turn of the century. You feel the fog on your skin, smell the combination of horse and horseless carriage and cheap coal in the air. You're there in these stories."

The Last Notes from the Dispatch-box of John H. Watson M.D. : Three Untold Adventures of Sherlock Holmes
Hugh Ashton
Published by j-views Publishing, 2018

ISBN-13: 978-1-912605-41-5
ISBN-10: 1-91-260541-4

j-views Publishing, 26 Lombard St, Lichfield, WS13 6DR, UK
publish@j-views.biz
www.j-views.biz

The Last Notes From the Dispatch-box of John H. Watson M.D.

Contents

The Last Notes From the Dispatch-Box of John H. Watson M.D.

Three Untold Adventures of Sherlock Holmes

Discovered and Edited by
Hugh Ashton

j-views Publishing, Lichfield, UK

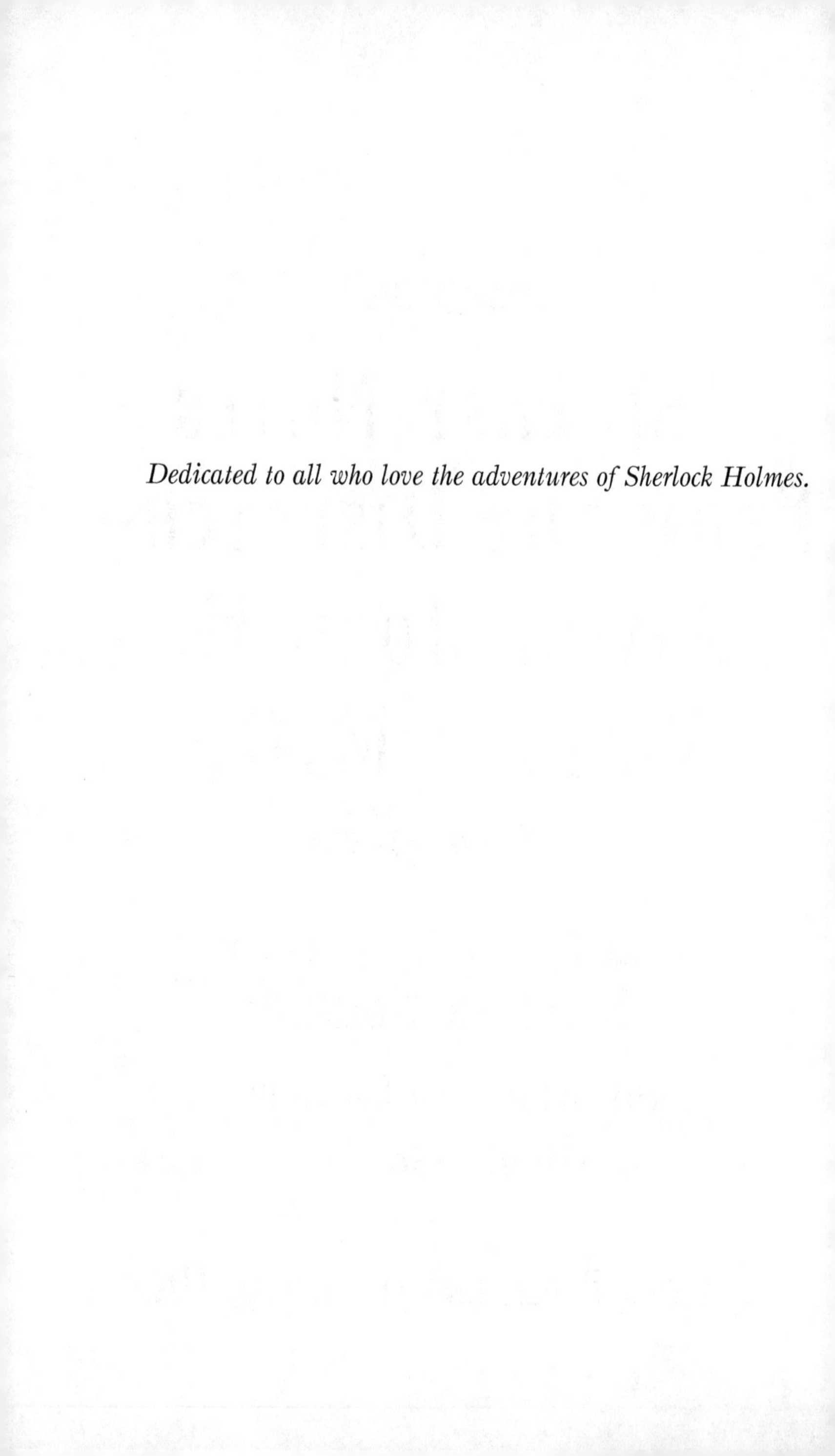

Dedicated to all who love the adventures of Sherlock Holmes.

Preface

T is with a sense of great sadness that I find myself looking at the bottom of that famous dispatch-box, the second such deposited in the vaults of Cox & Co. by Doctor John H. Watson, late of the Indian Army.

Two of the three adventures contained here, however, should prove of great interest to Sherlockians, the third being more of a trivial, if amusing, curiosity than an account of Holmes' battle against the criminal classes.

HE first of these, which was untitled by Watson, but which I have taken the liberty of naming "The Case of the Russian Bear", involves the British Government, as represented by Mycroft Holmes. The circumstances surrounding it are mentioned in "The Disappearance of Lady Frances Carfax", where Holmes mentions to Watson that it would be impossible for him to leave London while "old Abrahams" is in such danger. We are not told any more about Abrahams in the Canon, but he may be identified as Sir David Abrahams, who makes his appearance in "The Enfield Rope".

In it, we see Holmes' varied interests, including Kaballah, and some knowledge of the anarchist and revolutionary movements in Russia at the end of the 19th century (the last no doubt at least as the result of his work for Mycroft).

There can be little doubt in my mind that Watson witheld publication of this adventure on account of its political sensitivity.

HE second adventure recorded here, "The Hand of Glory", is a purely domestic adventure, taking place as it does in a small unnamed Warwickshire market town, which it is impossible to identify from the sketchy description here.

Holmes' knowledge of the esoteric superstitions of the past stands him in good stead here, and leads him to a satisfactory elimination of a criminal conspiracy, set up and masterminded for reasons of personal revenge.

The grisly elements in this story are beyond anything described elsewhere by Watson, surpassing even "The Cardboard Box" and "Black Peter" in their gruesome nature. It seems to me that this would form a reason for this adventure to remain unpublished by Watson.

ASTLY, we turn to the "Disappearing Spoon"; a light-hearted look at a very minor incident in which Holmes renders assistance to a former schoolfellow. Disappointingly, though, we are not informed which school he attended (my personal belief is that Holmes was educated at Stonyhurst College, but there is no way of verifying or disproving this from the material available here).

LTHOUGH these adventures have emptied the second box of Dr. Watson's papers to come my way, I do, however, live in hopes that there is more to come, and that Doctor Watson has left some more notes in a location yet to be discovered.

It would be a sad day indeed, were we to discover the last of Sherlock Holmes' adventures to be recorded, knowing it to be the last such.

Hugh Ashton
Kamakura, 2014

The Adventure of the Russian Bear

Y friend Sherlock Holmes was the possessor of a powerful intellect, allowing him to engage his faculties on more than one case simultaneously where the resolution of only one such would doubtless prove an insurmountable challenge for lesser mortals.

Nonetheless, on several occasions I have known him to gather up the tangled threads of several unrelated seemingly inexplicable sequences of events, and move from one to the other, solving each problem with as much ease as if it were the only occupation upon which he was engaged.

Add to this the fact that he was often also engaged in the composition of a musical piece for the violin, or research into one of the numerous topics that from time to time engaged his fancy, and you will have an idea of the kind of man I was proud to call my friend.

On one such occasion, I was away from London at Holmes' request, paying an extended visit to Lausanne in the matter of the Lady Frances Carfax. Holmes had remarked to me that he was unable to attend to the matter himself, due to the danger in which " old Abrahams" found himself. The gentleman in question to whom Holmes so cavalierly referred was Sir David Abrahams, the financier, with whom Holmes had struck up an acquaintance during the matter of the pearl necklace belonging to the Enfield family. It transpired that Abrahams and Holmes shared similar tastes in music for the violin, and such entertainments not always being to my taste, a fact of which Holmes was well aware, his chosen companion was very often Sir David, who was raised to the knighthood by the Prince of Wales soon after our initial acquaintance. Holmes was therefore engaged in the protection of his friend, as well as the investigation of Lady Frances, as well as on several other matters, the time for the revelation of which is not yet ripe.

I was living in with Holmes at the time, sharing the rooms in 221B Baker-street, leading the bachelor existence which

Holmes relished. The presence of Woman in our lives, save in the position of housekeeper, would have been abhorrent to his style of life. Undoubtedly she, had she existed, would have attempted to restore order from the seeming chaos which surrounded him, and thereby plunged his work into disorder. I knew for myself, from my well-meaning efforts to instil a little discipline into his work, that traditional notions of neatness and method were not for Sherlock Holmes, though it was with some reluctance that I tacitly accepted the Persian slipper, the coal-scuttle, and the other aspects of Holmes' peculiar ideas regarding housekeeping.

CCORDINGLY, we were sitting at breakfast one morning – though I say "sitting", Holmes' attitude might better be described as "lounging", as he reclined on the sofa as if on some Oriental divan, taking in his toast and eggs in a languorous manner, perusing the morning's post while clad in his dressing-gown.

"Bah! Sheer piffle, Watson!" he exclaimed, throwing one epistle into the fire, where it burned merrily. "The woman seems not to have the sense to see what is in front of her nose. The ring she has been given is a fake, and so is the betrothal. I have had enough of this sort of affair to last me several lifetimes." So saying, he picked up the next envelope in the pile, which I noted was of a somewhat less refined appearance than those comprising the rest of the morning's correspondence. "From old Abrahams, if I am not mistaken, from the writing. No doubt it contains the tickets for next Saturday's concert, which explains the strangeness of the envelope when compared to his usual choice of stationery." He opened the envelope and withdrew a single sheet of paper, at the sight of which his face fell. "I am sadly in error, Watson, not as to the writer, but as to the content. If I am to take this message seriously–and I have no reason to do otherwise–our friend is in some peril. See for yourself." He tossed the paper to me, and I read the following.

" 'My Dear Holmes,
Please accept this humble missive, for which I cannot
help but apologise. I hope that you will find it in you to forgive
me but I will be unable to join you on Sunday for Gaspari's recital,
as circumstances beyond my control have rendered it necessary that
I must decline the invitation. As you can readily imagine, I
am not happy that this unfortunate circumstance places you
in a position of considerable inconvenience which must cause
great disappointment.'
ראַפעג

" ' My Dear Holmes,

Please accept this humble missive, for which I cannot help but apologise. I hope that you will find it in you to forgive me but I will be unable to join you on Sunday for Gaspari's recital, as circumstances beyond my control have rendered it necessary that I must decline the invitation. As you can readily imagine, I am not happy that this unfortunate circumstance places you in a position of considerable inconvenience which must cause great disappointment.'

And then a word of letters that I take to be his signature in the Hebrew tongue. I see no peril here, though."

" And what do you make of the letter, in that case ? "

I was accustomed to this kind of inquisition, and studied the paper carefully. " It was written in haste, as can be seen from the way in which the pen has dug into the paper in places," I said.

" Good, Watson. You are coming on well."

Emboldened, I went on. " The paper is of a quality not usually employed for such communications. There is a strangeness about the formation of certain of the letters which may or may not be of importance. As to the Hebrew," I shrugged, " that is beyond me."

" An excellent summary of the obvious. It is true that you have missed most of the major points relating to this letter, but other than that, you may be considered to have done well."

I was somewhat nettled at this criticism. " What, in your opinion, did I overlook ? "

" First, you failed to note the significance of the paper, other than the somewhat trivial fact that it was unusual. It is a somewhat thick paper, of a coarse and fibrous nature, which as you pointed out, accounts for the pen digging in at times. However, the pen itself, if you will take the trouble to examine the strokes carefully, is not of the finest type. There is a slight nick from the tip of the nib which imparts a jagged quality to the downstrokes of the letters. Returning to the paper, I would say that it is butcher's paper, and has been torn, albeit neatly, from the corner of a larger sheet. You will see that two sides of the paper are cut, while the other two are torn, possibly using a ruler or some similar straight edge as a guide."

" But what does this mean ? " I asked.

" The answer lies in the letters you just described as ' strangely formed', and these letters here," he said, pointing to the strange Oriental script.

" And the other letters ? "

" Pish ! The first word of each line is written more boldly than the other letters, and therefore may be assumed to have a greater significance. Read out those words."

I scanned the paper again and read " Please ... help ... me ... as ... I ... am ... in ... great ... and then I cannot read the last word, as it is in Hebrew, which is a language unknown to me."

"It is unknown to me as well," said Holmes, calmly. "However, I know the meaning."

"How is this possible?"

"Because this appears to be to be not a Hebrew word, but rather one in the Yiddish language. A form of High German, with many Russian and Hebrew words, and written using Hebrew characters. Spoken by Jews in Europe, and familiar to men such as Sir David. I have sufficient knowledge of the Hebrew alphabet to be able to read the sounds from the letters, and sufficient knowledge of the German language to interpret the meaning."

"And that meaning is?" I examined the shapes shown below, but could make no sense of them.

ראַפעג

"I am reasonably certain that the word may be read as 'gefar', meaning 'danger'. It seems clear to me that Abrahams expected this letter to be read by other eyes than mine, and therefore wished to hide his warning, disguising it as a signature. He is well aware that I am conversant with the Hebrew alphabet as a result of the interest that I took at one time in the study of Kabbalah, and it was impossible for him to include the word in English without alerting those who were forcing him to write the letter. That he has been forced into writing the letter is surely indisputable, you will surely agree."

"So Abrahams is in danger, and wrote this message to you, attempting to disguise its true meaning?"

Holmes tutted in impatience. "We can assume nothing else, can we? I am of the certain opinion that this letter was written at the behest of those who would do him harm, and Abrahams being a man of some ingenuity, devised this method of communicating with me, trusting in my ability to discern his true meaning."

"A trust which was not misplaced," I said. "But the paper and the pen?"

"Obviously, this message was written while he was away from his home or his bank, or anywhere where he could expect to use his usual stationery. I know Sir David to be a man of some fastidiousness in such matters, and he would not have used such materials with which to write a letter unless there was some good reason for him to do so. I am certain that such an absence is involuntary."

"Of what nature do you consider this danger to which he refers to be?"

Holmes shook his head. "It is hard to make any kind of conjecture. I have heard nothing but good of the man and the way he conducts his business, and I have never seen him treat others other than with courtesy. It is hard to know what enemies he might have here in England."

"A kidnap for ransom, perhaps? He is a wealthy man."

"But who would pay the ransom?"

"He has no family in this country of which I am aware."

"His business associates, perhaps?" I ventured.

"A point well worthy of consideration. There may also be some relatives in Europe who are the target of the outrage I suspect of having occurred. However, I intend to find out more. I shall visit his bank this morning and talk with him."

So saying, Holmes replaced his coffee cup on the table, and strode into his bedroom, whence he emerged some minutes later, attired in overcoat and walking-boots. "You may expect me for luncheon," he informed me, as he left the room.

In the event, he was not present for that meal, and it was late in the afternoon before he returned, a look of puzzlement on his face. "I apologise for my non-appearance at luncheon," he said, flinging his hat onto the sofa, and throwing himself into the easy chair. "I have already made my apologies to Mrs. Hudson, who has promised to heat up the remains of the meal – ah, here she is," he broke off, as our landlady entered, bearing a tray and setting it down on the table. "Thank you," he addressed her, tucking in his napkin and falling to with an appetite that suggested his morning had been a strenuous one.

"But where have you been?" I enquired in some perplexity. "Was Sir David not at the bank?"

"Aye, there's the rub, Watson," he answered me. "I was not expecting to meet Sir David at his bank, but it was my first port of call nonetheless."

"He was not at the bank?"

"Correct. Not only was he absent from his office, but I was told that he had decided only yesterday to take a few days as a holiday, and had informed his partners there of the fact."

"He had informed them in writing?" I asked.

Holmes shook his head. "You make an excellent point, Watson. No, the information was transmitted by messenger as a verbal message yesterday morning. There was no letter such as we received. The messenger, I ascertained, was from a service that the bank had never used, and was unfamiliar to them."

"And the bank was unable to inform you of his whereabouts?"

"Once again, you are correct. I therefore took myself to Hampstead, where Abrahams maintains his bachelor establishment, but was unable to discover his whereabouts from his man or from his maids. According to them, he had set out for the City yesterday morning, and had not returned. A messenger had brought a note that afternoon informing them that he had to travel abroad on business and he should not be expected back for some time."

"A note? Written in Abrahams' own hand?"

"As far as I can judge, that is the case. I have it with me." He withdrew from his pocketbook a square of paper which appeared to be of the same type as that of the letter we had received earlier. "See here!" With an air of some triumph he fitted it to our earlier missive, and it was clear that not only had they been torn from the same sheet of paper, but that the torn edges fitted exactly. "We may assume, therefore, that Abrahams wrote, or to be more precise, was forced to write, these two letters, and possibly more, to persons as yet unknown, using whatever materials were to the hand of those who forced him. The timing of the delivery to his house and that of the message to the bank might well suggest that the message to the house, coming later, was an afterthought, as was the letter to us, judging by the time of the postmark." He picked up the envelope which had arrived on our breakfast table that morning, and scrutinised it. "Dear me, Whitechapel," he mused, examining the postmark. "Hardly a salubrious area where I might expect Sir David to be spending his days."

"Let us assume you are correct in your deductions," I said to Holmes, "in that Sir David is being held against his will in that area. How can you ever attempt to discover where he is being held, and who is holding him? It would appear to be a problem similar to the proverbial needle in a haystack."

Holmes smiled at my words. "You cannot believe that I spent the whole day on the two errands I have just described? I have spent a considerable time researching what I could discover of Sir David's past life before he came to this country. It is not easy, and the documents I required were, almost without exception, not written in English."

"Where would you find such records?" I enquired.

For answer, Holmes merely tapped his aquiline nose with a long forefinger. "These are matters about which you need have no knowledge, Watson, believe me."

I knew that his brother, Mycroft, had been described by my friend as being equivalent to the British Government at times, so I forbore from further enquiry.

"There is one other point to which I would draw your attention," said Holmes. "Compare the two letters; that addressed to me, and that to the bank."

I took the two pieces of paper and examined them. "They are clearly from the same piece of paper," I began, "as you observed. And quite possibly torn from butcher's paper, as you say."

"And your deductions from these observations?"

I shrugged. "I cannot say. Have you any theory?"

"Several at present, but there is none on which I would wish to pin my hopes as yet."

"How do you intend to pursue this matter further?"

"If my deepest suspicions are correct, I have little time to lose. I must take myself to Whitechapel at the earliest possible opportunity."

"Do you wish me to accompany you?"

Holmes considered this for a few seconds. "No, Watson," he replied. "Invaluable though your services are at times, I trust that you will not be offended if I say that this is one occasion on which I feel that you will prove more of a hindrance than a help. The mission I am about to take may well prove hazardous, and I have no wish to expose you to the dangers that may beset me."

"In that case, I must insist on accompanying you," I expostulated.

My friend shook his head. "No," he repeated. "You must remain here and act as my second line of defence. Should I fail to return within," he glanced at his watch, "six hours from now, that is, before midnight, I wish you to alert brother Mycroft, and, should my brother deem it necessary, Inspector Lestrade at Scotland Yard. Mycroft has some idea of the business on which I am engaged."

"And I do not!" I exclaimed bitterly. "Holmes, I had expected better of you than this."

"Peace, my friend," he replied. I fancied that his tones were not without some tenderness. "Believe me when I say that there are some things which it is better for you not to know at this stage. It is better for me, as well as for you, if you stay here and await my return, and act as my saviour should it become necessary."

I was a little mollified by this speech, and Holmes left me to change into attire more suitable for a visit to Whitechapel. Accustomed as I was to his powers of disguise, if I had not seen Holmes enter the bedroom alone, I would have taken my oath that it was a different man who emerged. The stage lost a fine actor when Sherlock Holmes took up the profession of detective, and it was not merely in his looks that he changed his personality. His movements, self-assured, but with an air of furtiveness, matched to a hair those of the unsavoury denizens of that area of the East End, and his voice and accents, when he spoke, were those of the most untrustworthy specimens of humanity infesting the East End of the metropolis. He could almost have stepped off the last boat from Riga, so perfect was the assumption of another's character. I could hardly forbear from applauding, so perfect was the performance.

" It is an act worthy of the finest theatres in London," I informed him.

" Aye, Watson," he answered me with a grim smile. " An act that, should it fail to please my audience tonight, may well cost me my life." So saying, he stepped to the bureau, and slipped the riding-crop with the weighted handle that formed his favourite weapon into his breast-pocket. " Watch well, my faithful friend," he told me. " Mark the clock, and if I have not returned before twelve tonight, Mycroft may be found at the Diogenes. He will know what to do and will instruct you accordingly." He turned in the doorway, and sketched a farewell salute, with his right hand brushing the greasy peak of his cap, before going down the seventeen steps leading to the door. I leaned out of the window to watch my friend, but the fog and dusk combined to prevent my following his path to the end of the road.

It was an anxious period that I spent in my wait for Holmes. On each occasion the quarter hour that the clock on the mantel chimed, I was reminded of the inexorable passage of time, and of the continued absence of my friend. The clock had struck its penultimate tune at a quarter before twelve, and I was preparing myself for the journey to the Diogenes Club, when Sherlock Holmes, still in his character of the Russian Jew, flung wide the door, a broad smile across his face.

" See the conquering hero," he exclaimed. " Bloody, but unbowed, as you may observe." He held up his right hand, the knuckles of which were indeed bleeding. " I fancy I gave back better than I received, however." He chuckled in a fashion that was not entirely pleasant to hear.

" You will permit me to dress your wounds, I hope," I told him.

" All in good time," he answered me in high good humour. " For now, brandy would seem to be an imperative, in order to wash the taste of that filthy beer from my mouth. Champagne would be a little premature, though I anticipate sharing a bottle with Abrahams before a few days have passed."

I made haste to pour a few fingers of cognac into a glass and handed it to him. " You know where he is, then ? "

" Better than that, " he said, draining the brandy at a draught. " I have seen him and spoken with him. The time was not right, though, for his release."

" But now you know where he is, is it not merely a matter of alerting the authorities and letting the police do the work for which they are employed ? "

Holmes shook his head. " Let me answer your question with one of my own. What do you know of the Okhrana ? "

" The name is hardly a familiar one to me, but I seem to recall that you have mentioned it in the past. It refers to the political police of Russia, does it not ? "

" Perfectly correct. Many of their officers are currently operating in London, especially in Whitechapel, where there is a concentration of poor outcasts who have fled from Russian persecution. Not all of these so-called refugees are what they might appear to be at first sight, however. Many of these are revolutionaries and anarchists who wish to further their nefarious ends while residing in an environment where they are less subject to police persecution. Though the authorities are well aware of their existence, and the goals which they seek, it is impossible for them to be apprehended, since they have committed no act which breaks the law of this country."

" But you are saying that the Russian police are encouraged to operate in this country?

Holmes smiled ruefully. " Their presence here is tolerated, rather than encouraged, and their activities are strictly curtailed by our own police. Observation is the limit of their powers here."

" But what has this to do with Abrahams? "

" It would appear, from my reading today, that Sir David was at one time in the employ of the Okhrana. Although as a Jew, he was not fully trusted by the authorities, he was employed as a kind of agent provocateur, joining some of the revolutionary groups, and urging them into committing an outrage which would then be communicated to the police in advance of the actual event."

" A kind of professional Judas, then? " I exclaimed in some disgust. " I had a higher notion of his morals."

Holmes wagged a finger at me. " My dear Watson, do I hear you aright? You are defending the rights of hoodlums and anarchists against the forces of law and order? "

I considered my words carefully before replying. " I think you know me well enough by now, Holmes, than to accuse me seriously of such sympathies. However, it seems to me to be an abuse of the trust reposed in a man to betray his comrades, however nefarious they may be."

"I understand your sense of duty and of loyalty, and I commend you for it. However, I would ask you to bear in mind that–and this information is imparted to you in the strictest confidence, you understand–Abrahams has single-handedly been responsible for saving the lives of at least one of the very highest members of the Russian Imperial family, through the timely warnings he passed to the authorities."

I pondered Holmes' words for a minute. "Very well," I admitted. "For now, I will accept your assessment. Who is holding him captive?"

"That is my problem at present. Though I was able to communicate with our friend through the small window of the cellar in which he is being held captive, he was unable to tell me anything of those who had taken him prisoner. All that he was able to tell me is that they were Russian, and that they appeared to him to be members of some of the organisations with which he had previous dealings." Holmes leaned forward, and spoke in a low and earnest tone. "Watson, I fear for our friend. Though he did not tell me, some of the matters he mentioned led me to believe that his captors will make a move against him within the next two days."

"What can you mean?"

"I believe that they will attempt to spirit him out of the country for their own foul purposes, or even to kill him here before they return to the Continent. He must be rescued from their clutches."

"But as I asked you earlier, why cannot the police be employed here? Why must it be you who carries out this task?"

"Because for them to do so would be to admit the presence of both these anarchists, and of the Russian secret police in this country. To admit the presence of either would deal a blow to the Government in the eyes of the public–a blow that must be avoided at all costs."

"I see the hand of Mycroft in all of this," I commented.

Holmes nodded soberly. "That is indeed the case. Though I am not acting under his orders, in the past he has made me almost painfully aware of his wishes in such matters, and those of the Prime Minister. It is therefore not for the police, but for me to act alone."

"I cannot permit you to carry out such a task unaided. Allow me to assist you in this matter. The matter is not one for you alone. It is for me as well," I retorted.

"There will be danger," he reminded me. "These are desperate villains."

"Pooh!" I retorted. "Have I not accompanied you on more hazardous adventures than these in the past?"

"And," he added, "should the guardians of the law discover us, we can expect no protection from that quarter. I may take it that you have no objection to sharing a cell with me for a number of years?" His words were serious enough, but his eyes twinkled.

"None whatsoever," I replied in the same vein as he himself had employed in speaking to me.

"Good man," he answered, leaning forward once more and clapping me on the shoulder. "You are, as ever, the one individual in whom I can repose the most absolute trust. We must make our move tomorrow. There is little time to be lost in this matter."

HE next morning, Holmes, despite his exertions of the previous day, was awake and breakfasting by the time I entered the room. He was dressed in a similar fashion to that which he had adopted for his visit to Whitechapel.

"You are too much of the 'toff'," he informed me curtly, after a glance at my attire. "If you really wish to be of assistance, please dress yourself in a fashion that will not attract undue attention. And prepare yourself for an extended walk to our destination. The use of a hansom would immediately rouse suspicion in our quarry."

It was not unknown for Sherlock Holmes to address himself to others so abruptly when his attention was claimed by the solution of a case in which he was involved, and I took no offence at his words to me or the tone in which they were uttered. I returned to my bed-room, and re-entered the sitting-room some minutes later, clad in clothes and footwear that I deemed more appropriate to the matter at hand. Holmes acknowledged the change with a wordless nod, and still without speaking, poured me a cup of coffee and helped me to eggs and bacon.

We sat in silence for some minutes, until I spoke. " Do you wish me to carry my revolver ? "

Holmes considered this for a few seconds. " I think not. It could cause the police to pay undue attention to us. A blackthorn, or failing that, your ashplant, will be sufficient, I believe."

" Very well," I answered him. " I will be happy to accede to your wishes in this regard."

" You will do well to remember," he reminded me once more as we set off, " that should we encounter opposition, we can expect no assistance from the authorities. Even Mycroft himself will be forced to disavow any knowledge of our activities."

It took us some considerable time to make our way on foot from Baker-street to Whitechapel, and I was heartily glad when Holmes led the way into a public house, though the establishment was hardly of the type that I would have selected under other circumstances.

" The beer here is of a quality that I have happily failed to encounter elsewhere," he whispered smilingly in my ear. " However, I advise you to drink it with as good a grace as you can muster."

The somewhat dirty glass that he pressed into my hand as he led the way to an isolated table in the corner of the room did little to inspire me with confidence, and the taste of the brew it contained was, as I had been warned, hardly to my taste, or indeed, to the taste of any man with a civilised palate.

Holmes sipped his beer with a nonchalance that I found it hard to emulate, and gazed around the room in a seemingly aimless fashion while he filled his pipe with a vile ship's tobacco. To all intents and purposes, he was one of the idlers who were partaking of the foul brew served in the place. His seemingly absent-minded actions would seem to have no purpose to those who lacked his acquaintance, but to me, familiar with his moods and gestures, he was in fact scanning the assembly of rough and ready characters for a significant sign.

Without any apparent change in his attitude, he spoke to me. " Finish your beer as quickly as you can, Watson. It would never do to leave any behind, as that would draw unnecessary attention to ourselves." He followed his own advice, swallowing the ale with enviable ease, and waited for me to follow suit before rising to his feet and sauntering in a leisurely fashion out of the door.

He walked briskly through the foul alleys that formed the streets in that part of London, seemingly heedless of the filth that surrounded us, and I did my best to stifle my natural repugnance as I followed him.

" Why did we leave the inn at that time in such haste? " I asked him as softly as I could under the circumstances under which we found ourselves.

He answered me in similar low tones. " I had observed two men whom I had previously noted as being Abrahams' captors enter the bar and purchase drinks. The coast, if not clear, is at least less heavily encumbered."

" But they will not be the only guards," I objected.

"To be sure, that is so. However, the odds will be slightly more in our favour, do you not agree, with two safely out of the way? Never fear, we have not much further to go," he added, viewing the fashion in which I was avoiding the foul messes covering our path. "Here," he hissed suddenly, looking all around, and having satisfied himself that we were unobserved, darted into a doorway located in a deserted alleyway.

"Do you loiter in the roadway and keep watch," he whispered to me, withdrawing his row of picklocks from inside his coat. "At the first sign of anyone approaching, whistle some tune such as the Londonderry Air."

I turned my back on him, and gazed anxiously up and down the street, listening to the sounds of Holmes struggling against the lock. After a mercifully short time, during which my nerves were stretched to almost breaking point, I heard a loud snap as the lock was freed.

"Now, Watson, now!" my friend hissed, and I followed him as swiftly as I could through the doorway into the darkened house, whereupon he shut the door behind us, leaving me temporarily unable to perceive anything. We paused and both of us strained our ears to determine if we were alone in the house. After nearly a minute's listening, or so it seemed to me, my friend grasped my arm. "Listen," he breathed. "Do you not hear it?" It seemed to me that there was more than a touch of humour in his voice, faint though it was. I listened hard, and could just hear a faint sound of snoring, seemingly proceeding from the first floor. I smiled to myself in the darkness. If two of our adversaries were refreshing themselves at the hostelry we had just departed, and the others were asleep, our task of rescuing Abrahams would be an easy one, it seemed to me.

"Follow me," Holmes commanded me in his breathless whisper. "Take hold of my coat-tails if you cannot see." My friend, who possessed an almost cat-like ability to make his way in the dark, led the way down the stairs to the cellar of the house, where a feeble light came from the outside through a grating. There I recognised, albeit with some difficulty, Sir David Abrahams, dressed in the remnants of what must have been expensive clothing, but now befouled and tattered almost beyond description.

"Thank God you are here again!" exclaimed Sir David. "I feared that you would be unable to return."

For answer, Holmes merely placed a finger to his lips.

"I understand," replied Abrahams, in a lower tone. "How many of my captors are here, do you know?"

"We do not know," Holmes told him in the same whisper. "How many are there in all, do you know?"

"I have seen but the three."

"Then there is only the one here," said Holmes, "and from the sound of him, he is fast asleep. "The other two are refreshing themselves at a nearby tavern. Come, let us go." He placed a hand under the other's armpit, and I took the other arm, and we attempted to raise him to a standing posture. Our efforts were foiled, however, by the chains, which had remained unnoticed by us, fastening the prisoner's wrists to a ring set into the wall. We therefore lowered him gently to his former sitting position, and Holmes brought out his picklocks once more. A few minutes' work and the shackles fell to the floor. As we raised Abrahams to his feet, with horror we heard the sound of the key rattling in the front door above us, and the door being opened, to the accompaniment of what appeared to be curses and oaths, though in a language unknown to me.

"They have returned!" exclaimed Abrahams.

"Never fear," Holmes reassured him. "Watson and I are ready to take on these men."

I gripped my ashplant firmly with my right hand, while supporting Abrahams as best I could with my left. Holmes had withdrawn his riding-crop from its hiding-place, and had moved to a position where he would be hidden when the cellar door opened.

We could hear the tread of heavy feet descending the steps, and the door-handle rattled, but our visitors seemed to be experiencing some difficulty in opening the door. I noticed that Holmes had quietly slipped two small wedges into the door-frame, effectively barring entry to intruders. There was a series of heavy thuds against the door as our visitors presumably launched an attack on it. After several of these assaults, the door suddenly sprang open, and a large heavily-bearded man crashed into the room, stumbling. Holmes swiftly stepped forward, and raised his riding-crop to strike his victim smartly behind the ear, whereupon he slumped to the floor, seemingly senseless.

My friend stepped forward to examine the body, but another man entered the room, a revolver in his hand, which was pointed directly at Holmes.

" You may put that down," he exclaimed in a guttural voice, gesticulating with the pistol at Holmes' weapon.

Holmes shrugged, and let the riding-crop fall to the floor. As his assailant's eyes followed its descent, I stepped forward, and dealt the ruffian a smart blow over the wrist with my stick. He let out a howl of pain and dropped the gun on the floor, from which Sherlock Holmes deftly retrieved it.

" I think we may leave now," he said to me. " Assist Sir David up the stairs, Watson, while I make sure that our friends do not follow us."

I did as requested, Abrahams proving to have a little more strength than had at first appeared, and Holmes followed, walking backwards up the staircase, the barrel of the revolver pointing steadily at our would-be assailant.

As we left the house, we could hear the sound of the third man upstairs. " Quick, Watson ! " Holmes said. " It is time we were on our way. Take this road," he commanded, pointing to the road opposite to the direction which we had taken to reach the house.

The brute who had threatened us with the revolver stepped out of the house as if to follow us, but a motion of Holmes' hand holding the revolver, added to the appearance of a small group of navvies at the end of the street, seemed to dissuade him from his intentions.

We hurried to a slightly more salubrious part of the city, and Holmes summoned a four-wheeler. After one glance at our tattered appearance, the jarvey was reluctant to allow us into his vehicle until Holmes produced a half-sovereign and demanded in his most commanding tones that we be taken to Baker-street.

Once there, we requested Mrs. Hudson to prepare a bath for Abrahams, and once he was cleansed of the filth that coated him, I proceeded to examine him for any signs of injury or illness, fortunately discovering none such.

Abrahams' own garments being in a state beyond repair, and he being closer to my size than that of Holmes, I clad him in some of my clothes, which fitted him tolerably well, and for which he expressed his sincere thanks.

In the meantime, Holmes had commanded a nourishing repast, and following my examination and his reclothing, Abrahams fell to with a hearty appetite. He had just finished eating when Mrs. Hudson knocked on our door.

" Pardon me, sir," she said to Holmes, " but there's a foreign gentleman to see you. Shall I show him in? "

" To be sure," answered Holmes, briskly rubbing his hands together. " I have a good idea of who this might be, and I look forward to meeting him."

" Very good, sir," replied our landlady, leaving us.

" Sir David," Holmes said in an urgent tone, " I strongly recommend that you lie on the bed in that room. I feel that this is an interview at which your presence would not be conducive to mutual understanding."

"I hardly comprehend your meaning," answered Abrahams, but he suffered me to lead him into the bed-room, where he lay on the bed.

As I re-entered the sitting-room, and closed the door behind me, there was a firm knock, repeated four times, on our sitting-room door. Holmes strode to the door and opened it.

"Welcome, Your Illustrious Highness," he greeted our visitor, a giant bear of a man, swathed, despite the weather, in a barbaric fur robe.

"Who is this?" I asked Holmes, as our visitor seemed disinclined to speak, contenting himself with a piercing glare which he directed at every corner of the room in turn.

"Our visitor is Count Alexei Alexandrovich Orloff, one of the Second Secretaries at Chesham House, that is to say the Russian Embassy, and the leader of those here in Britain working for the Okhrana."

"And you, my friend, must be the Devil himself that you know such things without a word being spoken," our visitor retorted in a deep rumbling voice which betrayed his surprise at Holmes' words. "My work with the Okhrana is known to few men."

"Then you must include me as one of that select company," replied Holmes suavely. "Your work in that area has not gone unnoticed by some."

A flush darkened the other's cheek. "I was not aware that my fame had preceded me so far." His tone was cold and brusque. "Maybe you also know why I am here today?"

"I assume that I am correct in my belief that you are in search of knowledge as to Sir David Abrahams' whereabouts and you think I may be able to assist you in that regard."

Our visitor bowed slightly in Holmes' direction. "I can tell that you are all that has been said about you. And the answer to my question?"

Holmes spread his hands. “ Alas, I am unable to inform you of his precise whereabouts, since his leaving Whitechapel.”

Fire flashed in the other’s eyes, but his voice remained steady as he spoke to my friend. “ Have a care, Mr. Holmes. You may think yourself safe now, but the time will come when you may regret your present insolence. I will ask you more directly : do you know the precise whereabouts of Sir David Abrahams at this time ? ”

“ I cannot answer your question,” Holmes answered him evenly.

“ In that case, I can only repeat my advice to you to have a care. Should you at any time in the future discover the whereabouts of our mutual friend, I believe you know where you may find me.”

So saying, the Russian retrieved his hat from the table where he had thrown it, and showed himself out of the room.

“ Well ! ” exclaimed Holmes, laughing. “ We certainly attract the cream of the crop, do we not, Watson ? ”

For myself, I was somewhat worried by the threats that had been uttered, and I said as much to Holmes.

“ Pish ! ” he answered me. “ Even were he or his minions to attempt any mischief, he knows well that such an attempt would not remain unpunished. He is well aware of the position that brother Mycroft holds, and of my relationship to him.”

We were startled by Abraham’s voice, coming from the bedroom, whose door was now slightly ajar. “ Do not be so sure of that, Holmes,” our guest said. “ Count Orloff himself may not be anxious to invite retribution on himself, but he will have no qualms about sacrificing his minions on the altar of revenge, should he feel sufficiently crossed in his path.”

“ Well, well, we can cross that bridge if and when we arrive at it,” replied Holmes, seemingly unconcerned by this possible threat to his safety. “ Our question now is how to keep you safe, Sir David."

"The bank can manage without me for some time," said Abrahams. "I hardly think that it is necessary for me to go into the office for a few days."

"Nonetheless, your bank and your home will be the main locations that they will be watching," Holmes told him. "It will be best for you to avoid these places until such time as the fangs of this snake have been drawn."

"It seems to me," I added, "that these rooms here in Baker-street likewise form a target for observation. But cannot Mycroft provide some protection for Sir David?" I asked. "Or even, given Sir David's links to a certain Royal personage, maybe the same measure of protection could be afforded to Sir David as to his Royal Highness?"

Holmes, who had appeared deep in thought, sprang up with a cry. "Why, Watson, you have it!" he exclaimed. "You have solved the problem of how to keep Sir David safe from the attentions of Orloff and his bunch of beauties." He crossed to the bureau and scribbled a few lines on a piece of paper before placing it in an envelope, and ringing the bell for Billy, our page. "Billy, take this message to my brother in Whitehall. The address is on the envelope, do you see? Give it into his hands, and to no-one else. Then wait for his answer, which you are to bring straight back to me. If anyone attempts to stop you, present my card to them. Do you understand me?"

On his giving an affirmative answer which pleased Holmes, Billy ran off, clutching the envelope and the card. I was full of curiosity as to what Holmes intended, but he was not to be drawn on the subject, instead discussing the art of the fiddle with Sir David as if the situation in which we currently found ourselves were a normal one, and Abrahams had simply passed by and decided on a whim to pay us a call.

For myself, unable to join in the conversation, the time passed slowly, and I stood up and observed the passers by from the window. After some time, a carriage drew up in the street below, and to my surprise, the page-boy Billy descended from it, followed by two soldiers in the uniform of the Guards. I drew Holmes' attention to the sight, and he rubbed his hands together with satisfaction.

"I have to confess that I hardly expected Mycroft to act so fast," he said, as the soldiers entered the front door of the house. Shortly afterwards, Billy led the procession into our rooms, proudly puffing out his chest as if he had been promoted to colonel of a regiment of the Guards.

The soldiers, a sergeant and a corporal, halted at attention. "Sir David Abrahams?" the sergeant enquired of our guest, who nodded, seemingly dumbfounded, in response. "If you will be good enough to come with us, sir?" As if in a trance, Abrahams rose, and, flanked by the two soldiers, made for the door. "Do you know where they are taking me, Holmes?" he asked.

"Indeed I do," smiled my friend. "And I have no doubt in my mind that you will find it congenial. Farewell. I may call upon you in a day or so."

I could hardly contain my curiosity as Abrahams and the soldiers entered the carriage, which drew away. Holmes was chuckling softly to himself as he saw my bewildered countenance.

"Where is he going?" I asked.

"Why, to Marlborough House, to stay at the residence of the Prince of Wales, who is currently in Biarritz. It was your words that gave me the idea. There is nowhere that old Abrahams will be safer than there, guarded by the cream of our Army."

"I had no idea that Mycroft possessed such influence," I said.

"Why, man, believe me when I say that this is a small part of the power he possesses. When Mycroft speaks, Prime

Ministers and Princes listen and take note."

"I am puzzled, though," I confessed to Holmes. "You told me that Abrahams had worked for the Okhrana. Why are they now pursuing him?"

"That is something I am unwilling to answer at present," he told me, "but we can hardly assume that the danger will disappear simply because Abrahams is safe. I cannot leave London at this time, given the danger he perceives himself to be in. It is a confounded nuisance, as there are rumours of a case on the Continent that demands my attention. Still, for a few days, I believe there is little useful that you or I can achieve in this regard."

"In that event," I said to Holmes, "I will take myself off for a few days. I may not be as old as some, but I am feeling in need of somewhat less strenuous exertions than have been the case recently. The twinges of rheumatism are creeping in and my wound starts to nag at me. In any event, I must ensure that my patients have not completely forgotten my existence."

"Anno Domini, Anno Domini," he laughed. "Perhaps I shall see you in two or three days when the joys of performing Hippocratic ministrations have worn off."

As it happens, it was four days before I returned to Baker-street, when the colloquy that I described at the beginning of the remarkable affair of the Lady Frances Carfax took place, which concerned my sharing a cab and partaking of the delights of a Turkish bath. As Holmes remarked at that time, it was impossible for him to leave London while Abrahams was in such terror of his life, and I therefore travelled to Lausanne alone, and thence to Montpellier, as described elsewhere. Despite Holmes' protestations that he could not leave London, he nonetheless travelled to Montpellier, where he proceeded to criticise my actions in no uncertain terms; in my opinion, somewhat unjustly.

However, I held my peace, and following the successful, if

somewhat macabre, resolution of the matter relating to the Lady Frances, my thoughts once again turned to Abrahams.

"Is he not still in danger?" I asked Holmes, after we had returned to Baker-Street.

"I persuaded him that the danger was not as serious as he believed, as long as he remains at Marlborough House."

"And you have heard nothing from Count Orloff?"

Holmes' countenance grew serious. "Not from the Count himself, but I have received attentions from his henchmen while you were blundering about the Continent."

I bit off the retort that sprang to my lips, and merely enquired as to the type of attentions that he had encountered.

"To be sure, they were clumsy attempts," he told me. "I was set upon by supposed footpads at one time, and I narrowly escaped being trampled by a team of horses in the Strand only the other day–an event which I cannot regard as being a mere accident. There was also the small matter of my returning to these rooms just before my remove to the Continent a week ago, and discovering the room filled with gas that had escaped from that jet there. Had I been smoking my pipe at the time, or had I been carrying a candle, I dare say that there would now be a small pile of rubble to mark the spot where this house had formerly stood. Naturally, I opened the window and cleared the air."

"And Mrs. Hudson saw or heard nothing?"

My friend shook his head. "She was absent on that evening, visiting her sister, and none of the servants will admit to having witnessed anything."

I confess to being more than a little mortified. "Why did you not tell me of this? I would be more than willing to assist you in this kind of matter, as you are well aware."

"I value your support, Watson, more than I can say, believe me. But with the best will in the world, we are up against some of the most ruthless villains of this type that can be imagined. However, the advantage is not all on their side. From the incident of the gas-jet onward, this house has been under the observation of the most skilful and discreet watchers of their kind."

"You refer to the Special Branch of the Metropolitan Police?"

"No," he smiled. "I refer to Wiggins and his gaggle of Baker Street Irregulars, who have been watching this house in shifts around the clock. Should they discover anything, they have standing orders to summon a constable, and to pass on a code word to Scotland Yard, which will alert Gregson and his men. However, nothing has transpired so far. It is now time to stop acting as the hunted, and to play the hunter. That, my dear Watson, is a role to which I believe you are better suited than that of victim-in-waiting." He smiled.

"You have a plan, then?"

"I believe so," he said. "It will involve some danger."

"That will present no problem to me," I told him. "As always, I am your man."

"Excellent. My plan is not to entrap those ruffians whose acquaintance we had the pleasure of making in the Whitechapel house, but to strike hard at the head; in other words, we must ensure that Count Orloff's position in this country is rendered untenable, and thereby deprive the Okhrana here of any authority. We must set a snare for him, baited with such a tasty morsel as he will not be able to ignore or refuse."

"Such as?"

"Myself," he replied simply. "Even you, Watson, would not present such a temptation as would I, who stole his prey from under his very nose."

"And how do you propose to ensure that it is he who is trapped, rather than our Whitechapel friends?"

"The occasion must be one where Orloff will be welcome, but his bully boys will not. Orloff is not a man to shrink from violence, and I have little doubt that he will be prepared to carry out personally whatever he deems necessary to ensure my removal." The cool way in which Sherlock Holmes expressed these opinions excited my admiration. There are few men of my acquaintance who could remain as calm and collected as my friend under such circumstances.

"And Gregson and his men will assist us?"

"No, they cannot do so. Such an action would smack too much of the agent provocateur, and would cause unseemly diplomatic friction with Russia, which is something we can ill afford at the moment, as I am sure you are well aware. No, this is something that must be handled by us two alone. Are you with me still?" he asked, leaning forward with his eyes glittering.

"How can you ever doubt me?" I replied with some heat. "You know well that I am ready to undertake these adventures with you."

"Many pardons, Watson. You are a friend in a thousand–nay, in a hundred thousand. I propose to spring my trap at the ballet."

"A form of entertainment to which you are hardly addicted," I smiled.

"It is true that my views in the past on the art have been somewhat less than complimentary," he acknowledged. "However, it is a way of passing an evening to which the Russian people seem to be particularly addicted, and I happen to know that a famous ballerina from Petersburg, Mlle. Bulkhanova, will be dancing the title role in *Swan Lake* later this week. It has been made known to me that Orloff is susceptible to the charms of this particular young lady, and we may confidently expect him to attend the performance that night."

"I still do not understand what you intend," I complained.

"No matter," he smiled. "All will be revealed."

The next few days passed with Sherlock Holmes seemingly uninterested in the case, spending much of his time engrossed in a study of the ancient Chaldean language. In the evenings, however, he went out, brusquely refusing my offers to accompany him, and returned late, several times after I had retired for the night. When I attempted to question him as to the destination of these nocturnal excursions, he simply shrugged his shoulders and held his peace.

At the end of the week he addressed me at breakfast, asking me whether I was engaged that evening.

"Hardly," I answered him.

"I had surmised as much. In that case, maybe you will do me the pleasure of accompanying me to Covent Garden this evening? Evening dress and a revolver would be appropriate for the occasion, I fancy. Be ready to leave at seven thirty. If all goes well, we may enjoy a supper at Alberti's after the performance." With that, he returned to the toast and coffee before him, and declined to answer any further questions.

At the appointed time, I was ready, and Holmes emerged from the bedroom, clad in impeccable evening dress, with an unaccustomed flower in his buttonhole. I remarked on this addition to his wardrobe, to which he replied with a smile that change was always welcome.

We made our way to Covent Garden, and seated ourselves in the stalls where Holmes had previously reserved our seats in the centre of the third row. Prior to the curtain rising, Holmes occupied himself by peering through his opera-glasses at occupants of the boxes on either side of the stage, pointing out to me those that he assumed would be of interest to me. In truth, the Earl of This and the Marquess of That held very little fascination for me, and I was somewhat at a loss as to why Holmes considered these people to have any appeal at all. Among those whom he pointed out was Count Orloff, who occupied a box reserved for use by the officials of the Russian

Embassy. "Excellent," I heard him mutter to himself as he lowered the glasses. "Excellent," he repeated, and rubbed his hands together.

At that moment, the lights dimmed, and the conductor appeared to applause. I confess that ballet is not my favourite form of entertainment. My ear for music is not keen, and I have to admit the way in which stories are told in ballet does not commend itself to me.

Nonetheless, the prima ballerina, Mlle. Bulkhanova, was of more than passing prettiness. Though perhaps a purist might not describe her as "beautiful", there was certainly that about her person which would make any man look twice at her. To my surprise, I saw Holmes gazing fixedly at her whenever she was on the stage, with what I would have sworn was a look of rapt adoration on his face, had I not known his aversion to the sex to be profound.

At one point, I happened to glance up at the Russian box, and saw Orloff shooting besotted glances at the stage, interspersed with angry looks directed at the oblivious Holmes–expressions of such ferocity, indeed, that I was grateful for the distance between our places and the box. Holmes appeared to be blissfully unaware of these attentions, and continued to fix his gaze on the stage.

In the interval, we proceeded to the theatre bar to refresh ourselves, and I beheld Orloff in the crush of people awaiting their turn to be served. He had not seen us, however, and I judged it to be better for us to leave the place before he saw us. I therefore advised Holmes of this, explaining that I had observed the violence of the looks directed by Orloff towards Holmes throughout the performance. To my dismay, Holmes not only ignored my words, but plunged into the crowd, seemingly making his way directly towards the Count.

I refrained from following him into the crowd, and therefore was unable to see for myself in incident that provoked a giant bellow of wrath, together with a Slavic oath, which could only have proceeded from Orloff. Following this, I heard two voices raised in altercation, one of which appeared to be that of Holmes.

At length, my friend emerged from the crowd, the nosegay in his buttonhole somewhat disturbed, and his dress in slight disarray. He was, however, smiling.

"Pardon me if we forego our refreshments," he said to me. "It might be somewhat inconvenient to procure them at present."

I confess that I had been anticipating the pleasure of a brandy and water to assist me through the second half of the performance, but I guessed that Holmes wished to avoid any further friction with Orloff, and assented to this renunciation.

We returned to our seats, and I endured the second half of the performance, which was, however, made more enjoyable by the sight of Mlle. Bulkhanova. As soon as the applause was dying away, Holmes plucked at my sleeve and hissed in my ear, "Come now, and follow my instructions precisely." His urgent manner and tone formed a strange contrast to the languid ballet-lover who had lounged beside me for the past hour, but I hastened to obey, without fully understanding the reason for this urgency.

"Do not concern yourself with your hat and coat and scarf at present," he warned me as we hastened out of the theatre. "Stand where I tell you, and take this." He handed me his police whistle. "You will know when to use it, I am sure. In the meantime, stand here," and he pointed to a small alcove in the wall of the alley beside the theatre.

"And you?"

"I shall be waiting here, by the stage door," he smiled.

"For the delectable Mlle. Bulkhanova?" I asked.

"Ah, so you, too, find her delectable? She does possess a certain charm, I suppose, to those whose tastes run that way.

Yes, I am going to wait for her, and for one other."

So saying, he took up his station by the door and waited. As he did so, I heard the ring of heavy footsteps echoing along the alley.

"Not a word," Holmes hissed to me. "Attempt to conceal yourself as best you can and keep the whistle to hand. Blow it with all your might when I request you to do so, or when it seems prudent to you to use it."

I shrank into the shadows, as the massive figure of Count Orloff swaggered into view. He stopped short when he beheld the figure of Holmes, elegantly lounging against the doorway, and smoking a cigarette.

"What are you doing here?" he growled.

"I am waiting for a friend," my friend replied pleasantly, "as I suspect are you. May I offer you a cigarette?" He held out his cigarette case to the Russian, but it was waved away brusquely. "Very well, if you will not." He replaced the case, and continued smoking nonchalantly.

"May I ask for whom you are waiting?" asked Orloff.

"Oh, you may ask freely. However, I am under no obligation to supply you with the answer, I believe. However, I fancy that we are waiting for the same person."

"We shall see," snarled the other, and took up his post on the other side of the doorway, ostentatiously avoiding the sight of his rival.

At length, the stage door opened, and many of the members of the corps de ballet appeared, chattering and giggling like so many schoolgirls. Holmes and Orloff scanned the crowd, but it was plain that the object of their search was not numbered there.

A few minutes after this, the door opened again, and Mlle. Bulkhanova appeared, dressed simply but elegantly, and carrying a large bouquet of orchids. At the sight of her two admirers, she stopped and looked from one to the other with an air of amusement.

"I am flattered by your attentions, Your Illustrious Highness," she addressed the Count in accented, but clear English. "My company for this evening is, however, claimed by this gentleman here," motioning towards Holmes, "who has presented me with these flowers, and who has so kindly offered to escort me to supper." So saying, she moved towards my friend, and offered her arm to him.

The effect upon the Russian was nothing short of dramatic. Even by the light of the stage door, it was clear that his colour changed, and he started to breathe heavily. He spat out some angry words in Russian, to which she replied with a few in the same language, but uttered in a tone of sweet reasonableness.

He responded by moving forward, seizing her arm with one hand, and raising the other as if to strike her, but Holmes moved faster than the Russian, seizing the raised wrist of his opponent, and simultaneously gripping the other in such a way that Orloff cried out in pain and relinquished his hold on the ballerina.

"I will make you suffer for this," Orloff hissed at Holmes through his clenched teeth. "And believe me, I have much experience in making others suffer."

"I have no reason to doubt you," replied Holmes lightly. "The name of Alexei Alexandrovich Orloff is well-known among those seeking to free themselves from the tyranny of the Tsar's rule."

"They are but socialist and anarchist scum," spat the Russian. "They howl like dogs when I have worked my will on them, as will you in a few minutes, Mr. Sherlock Holmes, when you have felt the benefit of my attentions. Stand aside, Mademoiselle. Indeed, I would advise you to leave. The sights and sounds I anticipate are not for delicate ears such as yours. Ah, do not!" he interjected as Bulkhanova raised her hand to slap his face. He caught her by the wrist once more, bearing it down as she winced in pain. “ Leave us. It would pain me to use further force, so I am merely advising you to take yourself back into the theatre. Good girl,” he said, as she re-entered the stage door. “ And now, Mr. Holmes,” advancing on my friend, “ this is a pleasure I have been promising myself for some time now. Tonight’s little adventures have merely served to whet my appetite.”

His massive hands reached out as if to encircle my friend’s throat, but Sherlock Holmes deftly stepped aside and avoided the grip. As he stepped backward, however, he appeared to stumble and trip, and Orloff’s mighty fist crashed down on his head. I did not wait to see more, but faced along the alley to the street, blowing the police whistle as hard as I could. Happily, two constables happened to be passing at the time, and when I breathlessly explained the situation to them, they sprang into action.

I followed, to see Orloff bending over the prostrate body of my friend, and I feared the worst. Ignoring Orloff and the constables, I dropped to my knees, and anxiously examined Holmes’ pulse and breathing. I was relieved to discover that he was not only alive, but conscious, as he opened his eyes, and essayed a faint smile. “ Good man, Watson,” he said. “ Your sense of timing, as always, is impeccable.”

“ But you are hurt ! ” I exclaimed.

“ A mere love-tap,” he smiled. “ Listen to what our friend has to say.”

Above our heads, Orloff was expostulating to the policemen that he was a diplomat, and was not to be arrested, and that in any case, he had only been coming to the assistance of the man whom he had witnessed trip and fall. Here he indicated Sherlock Holmes, who had been listening to this farrago of lies with a sardonic smile on his lips.

“ Is this what happened, sir ? ” asked one of the policeman of Holmes.

"By no means," he told them, giving an account of the events that I had witnessed, to which Orloff listened with obviously mounting indignation.

"It is a fairy-tale!" exclaimed the Russian. "A pure fiction, caused by the blow to the head that he suffered when he fell, the poor man. You cannot take his word against mine, a loyal servant of His Imperial Majesty the Tsar of All the Russias."

"You would make an excellent point, Count, had I indeed fallen and hit my head in the way that he described to you just now. However," turning to the constable, "I do not ask you to take my word against his, but rather take the word of my friend Doctor Watson, late of the Indian Army, who witnessed the whole affair."

"Is that the case, sir?" the police officer demanded of me. "Which of these gentlemen's stories should we believe?"

"The events I witnessed are those described by Mr. Sherlock Holmes here," I declared stoutly. "Count Orloff's story is, I am sorry, to say, a tissue of untruths. Mademoiselle Bulkhanova, the dancer, will be able and willing to corroborate the first part of my story, I am sure."

Orloff's face grew black, and he snarled, "In any event, I am a diplomat. The law cannot touch me."

"You are now speaking the truth," Holmes admitted. "But I would advise you not to chance your arm and to make your way back to the Embassy as soon as possible."

"The gentleman is right, sir," said the constable to Orloff. "With the greatest respect, you are better off with your own people while this investigation is going on."

"What investigation is this?" snorted the diplomat, indignantly. "Very well. I bid you a good night, gentlemen." He strode off, having placed a sardonic emphasis on the last word of his speech.

"How are you, Holmes?" I asked anxiously when Orloff

had gone.

"I have seen better days," he smiled ruefully, "but I have also been in worse shape in my time. Do not concern yourself overly about me. I will sport a large bruise for the next few days, but I do not think there is any further damage. Of course, when we return to Baker-street, you are welcome to exercise your professional skills, but for now, we must to the Diogenes."

Both policemen expressed their concern as to Holmes' health, but he shrugged off their worries. "Watson here is a doctor," he assured them. "Should anything untoward befall me, I am in the best possible hands. Come, Watson, let us collect our coats and hats, and visit Brother Mycroft."

Mycroft Holmes received us in the Strangers' Room of that curious establishment, the Diogenes Club, where silence is enforced, and conversation prohibited between its misanthropic members. He listened to Holmes' account of the events, and pursed his great lips.

"It will be a pleasure to declare Orloff *persona non grata* and to send him out of the country," he told us. "Such an assault as you describe on a British citizen would be perfectly adequate grounds for this. The notice will be sent to the Embassy first thing tomorrow morning, and he will be out of the country within forty-eight hours."

"And the Okhrana apparatus in this country will fall to pieces," added his brother.

"It will indeed. The Russians will realise that we will not tolerate men such as Orloff to operate here, and they will be unable to replace him with anyone acceptable. You have successfully removed a thorn from the flesh of the British Government, Sherlock. The Prime Minister and the Foreign Office will be delighted."

HEN we returned to Baker-street, I was able to make a more complete examination of my patient, and discovered nothing untoward. I therefore advised complete rest for a few days, but had little expectation that Holmes would obey my instructions in this matter.

As it turned out, he was somewhat more amenable than I had anticipated, and the next morning saw him sitting up, breaking his fast in bed, a state of affairs almost unknown in my experience.

As I sat by the bed, I could not forbear from asking him a few questions.

" When did you establish that Abrahams' captors were the Okhrana and not the anarchists ? " I asked him.

" Oh, that much was immediately obvious from the letter that we received," he replied.

" How so ? "

" If you remember, the word for danger was written in Yiddish, in the Hebrew alphabet," he reminded me. " If the letter had been read by one of his erstwhile confederates, many of whom are Hebrews, they would have understood instantly. The Okhrana, as well as setting themselves against the would-be reformers in Russia, also despise the Hebrew race, so much so that they would scorn to learn even the basics of the language used by the Russian Jews. Abrahams therefore considered himself to be safe in using the Hebrew script, and therefore I concluded that he was held by the Okhrana."

" But why ? " I asked. " If he was guilty of double-dealing with regard to his colleagues and comrades, would it not be they would seek revenge ? "

" It appears," said Sherlock Holmes, shaking his head, " that Abrahams was guilty of more than double-dealing. In fact, he was guilty of triple-dealing. Those comrades whom he betrayed to the Okhrana were, it appears, double-agents themselves, and Abrahams was single-handedly responsible for the elimination of over twenty Okhrana agents. Do not judge him too harshly, Watson. You have seen for yourself what manner of man takes charge in that organisation, and believe me, Orloff is far from being the worst."

I in turn shook my head. "It seems strange that a man who is now a pillar of the City and an intimate of His Royal Highness should have such a background."

"He is little different from the ancestors of some of our own nobility," smiled Holmes, "whose fortunes were often made through treachery and violence."

I was ruefully forced to agree with this analysis. "I suppose," I said to Holmes, "that on the evenings that you went out without me, you were courting Mlle. Bulkhanova?"

"That is correct, in a sense. I had intended to play the part of a suitor and to deceive her into believing in my love for her. However, it rapidly transpired that she had no love for Orloff, either for the man himself, or for the wrongs he had inflicted upon her family. One brother of hers was exiled to Siberia, unjustly, she claims, and I have little reason to disbelieve her in this. Once I had explained my purpose to her, she willingly fell in with my scheme to deceive Orloff in the existence of a liaison between us. I found her to be a most pleasant and charming companion, and we did indeed spend a few enjoyable evenings together at the Café Royal."

"And the aim was to goad Orloff and provoke him into some rash act that would result in his expulsion from the country?"

"Precisely. You played your role to perfection, Watson. You allowed yourself to witness one criminal act and then brought the force of the law to bear with exquisite timing. The brute ceased his beating of me as soon as he heard the sound of the whistle, doubtless recognising that he would soon be confronting the forces of British law and order. But without your acting as a witness, it would merely have been his word against mine. As the archetype of a solid Englishman, your words turned the scale."

"I am glad to have been of some service to you," was the only answer I could make.

"More than merely 'some service', Watson!" he cried. "You rendered me invaluable assistance when it was most needed. I can never forget that."

I was saved from further embarrassment by a knock on our outer door, and Mrs. Hudson announcing a visitor.

"That will be the messenger from the Foreign Office, I expect," said Holmes, "bringing news of the decree against Orloff."

As it turned out, it was not. To my surprise, the petite form of Mlle. Bulkhanova graced our doorway, and she hesitantly enquired, in accented French, after the health of Sherlock Holmes.

"I am well, my dear," replied Holmes, now clad in his dressing-gown, from the bed-room doorway, replying in the same language. "Pray enter, and take breakfast with Watson and me. Ah, my manners. Mlle. Bulkhanova, my friend and biographer, Doctor Watson. Watson, Mlle. Bulkhanova."

"*Enchanté*," I replied, somewhat tongue-tied.

And so it was, that for the first and only time in my life, I shared a breakfast table with a prima ballerina and the world's foremost consulting detective.

The Adventure of the Hand of Glory

F all the adventures that I shared with Mr. Sherlock Holmes, few were more grotesque, to my mind, than that which I have described here. It started with a visit from a client whose first request regarding the matter of fees, while not a common one made of my friend, was one that was certainly not unknown to him.

It was made by a young woman, fashionably dressed, albeit in the fashion of one or two years previously, who had previously requested an appointment by letter, and Sherlock Holmes had granted her the favour of an audience, if it may be termed thus.

"I have to tell you, Mr. Holmes, that my sister regards my visit to you as a waste of my time," she began her interview. "I have left my sister in the hotel in Northumberland-avenue. We are here to see the sights and to pay a visit to friends in Town for a few days."

"And your sister also feels that your visit here to be a waste of your money," he added with a smile.

"Why, yes, that is so," she replied, starting. "I must confess to you that since my mother's re-marriage, our circumstances have been a little more strained. Indeed, my first question to you was going to be regarding your fees. If the figure that you mention is not one that can be easily encompassed within my budget, then I am afraid I must leave you, and make my apologies for having wasted your time."

Holmes leaned forward and smiled encouragingly. "My dear Miss Devereux," he said. "Watson here will be the first to inform you that are some cases that I take for the love of art, rather than financial reward. If you will do me the goodness to tell me your story, I will then be able to inform you whether your case is one of that category. Somehow, I suspect that it will turn out to be of that type." Having demanded and received permission to smoke, he lit his pipe, and settled back in his arm-chair as she related her tale to us.

"My name, as you know, is Mary Devereux. The family of my late father, John Devereux, is one of the oldest in Warwickshire, and while he was alive, our situation might well be regarded as one of comfort, if not of luxury. My elder sister Eliza and I, his only children, were given a good education and wanted for nothing. Three years ago, I lost the best of fathers, following a hunting accident in which his horse failed to clear a fence."

At this point, she produced a handkerchief and dabbed at her eyes, and Holmes and I looked away in some embarrassment. After a minute or so, she collected herself, and resumed her narrative.

"His estate was in order, and for the next two years, our material situation was unchanged. However, my mother met a man who attached himself to her, or rather, to her fortune–I can think of no other way of describing the relationship–and she married him a little under a year ago."

"The gentleman's name?" enquired Holmes.

She flushed a little. "It may seem churlish, but I would hesitate to describe Mr. Lionel Soames as a gentleman. To be sure, he can behave with a certain dignity, and he is dressed as he should be, but his choice of companions is far from what I would expect from a gentleman."

"How does he make his living?"

"That, Mr. Holmes, is one of the matters about which I wish you to make enquiries. It is something in the City, I believe. He leaves our house in Warwickshire every Monday morning, and returns some time in the week, usually on a Wednesday or a Thursday. He never talks about his work in London, but whatever it is that he does, it has taken large quantities of the money that was left to my mother and my sister and myself. We are by no means poor at present, but our fortune is considerably reduced, and if this diminution continues, poverty will be the end result in a relatively short time."

"Your father's money was not placed in trust for you?"

She shook her head. "No, it was left without reservation or entail to my mother. There is no obligation on her to pass it on to my sister and me. And that man has taken it, for what purposes, I know not."

"Has he behaved badly towards you or your mother? You mentioned that his interest in her was chiefly on account of her money."

Again, our fair visitor shook her head. "No, I cannot complain of his conduct towards us, or my mother, though he could never be described as a loving husband. It is his choice of associates to which I chiefly object."

"You mentioned them before–perhaps you can furnish me with some sort of description of them."

"If I have my doubts about Mr. Soames' being a gentleman, I have no doubts at all about the status of these rough men. They speak with uneducated accents, and their clothing is not that of men who have prospered. Indeed, some of them do not even wear a collar."

"And he invites them to your home?"

"He does. Two or three of them, never more, arrive late in the evening, almost always on a Friday, and I believe that they stay, drinking and smoking, often until the small hours of the morning, long after the household has retired. My stepfather has never introduced us to them, and nor would I desire such an introduction."

"You hear them leave the house? They do not spend the night there?"

"There have been many times when I have been awakened by the noise of their departure using our carriage. We live close to the market town, and I have no doubt that they stay at one of the inns there."

" You say that they depart using your family's carriage, although the servants have retired for the night, though you live close to the town ? "

" Yes, my stepfather acts as the coachman, it would seem. On more than one occasion when I have been awakened by the noise, I have looked out of my window, and seen the carriage depart, with my stepfather on the coachman's seat."

" And it is the same men on every occasion ? "

" As far as I can ascertain, yes. The same two men appear each Friday."

Holmes considered the information without speaking for a few minutes, while Miss Devereux appeared to be nervously awaiting his answer. At length he broke the silence. " Then you wish me to investigate Mr. Lionel Soames and his business, especially that relating to these mysterious nocturnal visitors ? "

" If that were all, Mr. Holmes, I fear I would be wasting your time."

" Hardly that, Miss Devereux. The case as you have described it would appear to have several points of interest. There is more, then ? "

" Indeed there is," she told us, and her voice rose in pitch in what appeared to be near-hysteria. " Grafton and Kimble are in our house at present, and neither I nor my sister wishes them there."

I broke in. " Grafton and Kimble ? " I asked. " Why, those are the names of the two housebreakers and murderers who were hanged at Pentonville not two weeks ago."

" Those are the men," she confirmed. " It is horrible ! Horrible to think that they are with us at our home." Again she buried her face in her handkerchief and did not speak for some time, during which her bosom rose and fell, obviously under some strong emotion.

" You must explain yourself a little, Miss Devereux," said

Holmes. “If these are the men to which Dr. Watson has just referred, I fail to comprehend how they can be staying with you.”

“My step-father claimed their corpses from the prison authorities, there being no next of kin. He promised to provide funerals and a burial for them, and had them transported to our house, where they were placed in the icehouse, where they reside still.”

Sherlock Holmes leaned forward. “How did you come to discover all this?”

“I was awakened late one night by the sound of wheels on the gravel drive outside our house. I arose, and drew aside the curtain to discover what was amiss. I saw the carriage carrying the coffins draw up outside our house, and the coffins carried in by the coachman and Mathews, my stepfather’s valet. The next morning, I persuaded Mathews to inform me of what had occurred the previous night, and he informed me that the coffins had come from Pentonville. More than that he could not, or would not, tell me.”

“The persuasion was of a monetary nature?” asked Holmes.

Miss Devereux blushed. “Like master, like man,” she said. “Both suffer from the sin of avarice. In any event, having obtained this information from George Mathews, my next step was to write to the Governor of the prison, asking him for further details, and he furnished me with the names of the criminals whose corpses had been sent to us, together with the details regarding my step-father’s promises.”

“And you have not asked your step-father about this?”

“I dare not,” she replied simply.

“When did the bodies arrive?” asked Holmes.

“Not one week ago,” she informed us. “Last Friday, to be precise.”

“And it is now Wednesday. Is your step-father presently in Town?”

" To the best of my knowledge, he is. At least, he is not at home, otherwise I would not have come here today."

" I take it that you have not viewed the bodies since their arrival ? "

She shuddered, and closed her eyes. " How could I do such a thing, Mr. Holmes? The very thought of such an action is repugnant to me."

Very well," said Sherlock Holmes. " Your case is indeed of considerable interest to me, and I am happy to take it on–at no charge," he added, seeing an expression of concern in her face. " Your address is on your card. I take it I may telegraph to you there should I require further information on the matter or should I discover anything that may be of interest to you ? "

Her face flickered with a look of anxiety, which passed so quickly that I was unsure as to whether I had imagined it. " Please address any communications in the care of my poor friend, Lydia Scythorpe, at the Vicarage. Here is her address. I would not like my step-father to learn that I have been in communication with you." She passed a scrap of paper over to Holmes, who in turn passed it to me.

" Very well, Miss Devereux," said Holmes. " I will be happy to do as you say."

I helped Miss Devereux to the street, and hailed a cab to take her to Euston Station. When I returned to our rooms, Sherlock Holmes appeared not to have moved from his chair, but was sitting with his eyes closed. Without opening them, he addressed me.

" Look out the Who's Who for two years ago on the third shelf of the right-hand book-case," he commanded, " and refresh my memory as to the details concerning the late John Devereux."

I located the requested volume, and made the search. " We were not told everything by our visitor," I informed Holmes.

"What piece of information have you just discovered?"

"We were informed that there is an elder sister, were we not? Eliza by name."

"Indeed so."

"I recall no other offspring of the late John Devereux being mentioned, and yet this volume refers to a son, Gerald, aged between the two sisters."

"Hmph. It is indeed strange that he was not mentioned in the narrative," reflected my friend. "If, of course, he is still alive," he added.

"I feel that she would have included the fact of his death in her recital, were that to be the case."

"It is certainly not a circumstance that would slip one's mind, to be sure. Was there anything significant that you observed about her appearance?"

"Her costume was costly, but not of today's fashions."

"I will take your word for that," he laughed. "I lack your detailed knowledge regarding such matters. We might, however, put that down to her living in the provinces, rather than London. You failed to mark her newspaper, then?"

"I noticed that she was carrying a newspaper in her bag, yes."

"But you noticed nothing else?"

"I did not."

Holmes sighed. "How many times must I impress upon you, Watson, the importance of details? It was open at the financial page, and was covered with pencil markings, almost certainly made by her today, since it was this morning's edition, and she claimed to have come up to London today. The implication is that although she is claiming poverty, of a relative kind at least, it cannot be so severe that she is unable to invest on 'Change. There is also the question of her jewellery. No doubt you remarked the ring that she was wearing?"

"I noticed it."

“ Two carats at the least, my boy, and of the finest water. Such a stone is worth several hundred pounds at the least. If Mr. John Devereux’ estate has been plundered significantly, I feel it must have been substantial to start with. Unless, of course,” he added, “ there is some other reason for her visit.”

“ Can you consider any other reason ? ”

“ Any number,” he replied airily. “ For example, though there may be no significant loss of money, there may be a loss of affection from the mother to the daughter. There is also a definite revulsion against the new step-father and his doings. It seems to me that Miss Devereux would be happy to see the last of him as a member of the household. The whole business, on her part at least, may prove to be no more than a simple tug o’ war, if I may term it so, of domestic affections.”

“ But you will take the case ? ”

“ Oh, indeed. I have every intention of so doing. The acquisition of the corpses of two hanged murderers is, after all, a matter that one does not encounter every day, and adds a deliciously macabre and outré flavour to the business.”

“ For what purpose would one acquire such grisly relics ? I can conceive of none, outside the medical profession, that is.”

“ Again, there are several alternatives that present themselves to my mind, but it would be premature to give preference to any at this stage,” he retorted. “ Before we make our way to Warwickshire, there are a few points about which I wish to satisfy myself. I take it that you will be accompanying me tomorrow ? ”

“ Naturally,” I replied. “ The case certainly promises to be of some interest.”

“ More than you might imagine,” he added enigmatically, before taking himself off on his errands.

He returned some hours later with a smile on his face. “ I am a little closer, perhaps, to the solution of the mystery,” he told me. “ Much may depend on Mathews.”

" The valet ? " I asked.

" The same."

He would say no more about the case that day, and the following morning, we set off on our journey to Warwickshire. Alighting at the small country market town, little more than a village, that Miss Devereux had mentioned to us, we discovered that there was but the one inn, the King's Arms. " No doubt this is where Mr. Soames' mysterious nocturnal visitors spend the night when they make their Friday visits," remarked Holmes.

" And today is Thursday," I reminded him.

" Indeed it is," he said. " Let us take our room, and then, I think, a call on the local vicar is in order."

However, when we knocked on the door of the Vicarage, we were informed by the maid that the Reverend Scythorpe was not at home.

" Would it be possible for us to talk to Miss Lydia Scythorpe, in that case ? " enquired Holmes, passing over his card.

" I'll see if she wants to talk to you," was the abrupt answer, at which Holmes and I exchanged smiles, once the door had closed and the maid departed on her errand. It was a matter of less than a minute before she returned with the news that " Miss Lydia would be delighted to see Mr. Holmes and Dr. Watson".

We were shown into a comfortable sitting-room, in the centre of which stood a tall, somewhat ungainly young woman of unprepossessing appearance, indeed, she might be described as being ill-favoured in her looks, and perhaps a little older than her friend. However, her smile of welcome seemed genuine enough, and the voice in which she greeted us was soft and melodious.

" I am so glad that dear Mary has retained your services," were her first words after the introductions had been performed. " It was I who recommended you to her, having read so much about you and your wonderful successes."

Praise of this type was always welcome to Sherlock Holmes, and he smiled at our hostess. "Miss Devereux has informed you of her troubles?" he asked.

"To which do you refer?" came the reply.

"Why, the troubles with her step-father, Mr. Soames," answered Holmes, blandly.

"Oh," she answered with a little laugh, which sounded incongruously, given the subject under discussion. "I had thought she had taken some advice from you about her brother."

Holmes and I exchanged a glance, and it was Holmes who replied. "Miss Devereux never mentioned a brother," he told her.

"How very strange. Mary was devoted to Gerald right up to the time of his de— disappearance." She stopped suddenly, and put a hand to her mouth. "I am sorry. I should not have said anything about the subject. If you will do me the kindness of forgetting what I have just said, or at any rate, not mentioning it to Mary, I would be very grateful."

"Very well," said Holmes. "I give you my word that she will never know from me that you have told us of this." I likewise promised my silence, and Holmes invited Miss Scythorpe to continue with her account of the step-father.

"Mr. Soames is an exceedingly handsome man," she began, and blushed a little. "I know that may appear a strange sort of introduction to the description of a man, but it is his most notable characteristic. As a person, he is pleasant enough, I suppose, but I would have to admit that there is little in his character beyond this initial pleasing nature."

"You consider that Miss Devereux' mother married him on account of his looks?"

"Chiefly on account of them, I would say."

Holmes raised his eyebrows almost imperceptibly. "I

am somewhat surprised that a mature woman such as Mrs. Devereux would solely be influenced by a man's looks."

"Not solely," she answered him. "As I said, he possesses some charm of his character. I know that Mrs. Devereux was desolated when her husband died, and was almost inconsolable in her loss."

"How did she come by his acquaintance, do you know?"

"I believe they met at a dance at Lord Southport's. It was the first such entertainment that she had attended since her husband's death, and I fear that the excitement of meeting him went to her head."

"Speaking of heads, yours would appear to be a particularly sound one," Holmes remarked. "You seem to be well acquainted with the vagaries of human nature," he smiled.

"I have some confidence in my judgements, Mr. Holmes," she said to him firmly. "Since my mother died some years ago, I have been assisting my father in parish work, as well as working among the poor in the nearby city, and I have come to an understanding of many of the facets of human nature that one encounters in life. Maybe my experience is not as broad or as deep as yours, but I assure you that I am seldom mistaken in my judgements."

"Quite so. What can you tell me of Mr. Soames' valet, Mathews?"

"A most unpleasant looking man," she replied. "Indeed, though a villainous face may often hide a virtuous heart, in the case of George Mathews, I find it hard to feel any charity or goodwill towards him. His scarred face, and general disfigurement would make him an object of pity, were he to conduct himself in a fashion one might term civilised." Seeing Holmes' expression of enquiry, she went on, "He does not return greetings addressed to him, and there are several other social niceties that are sadly lacking from his composition. If you wish to make his acquaintance, you may discover him in the public bar of the King's Head on most evenings, I believe."

"Why, that is where we are lodging," I exclaimed.

"Does Mr. Mathews favour the hostelry with his custom on Friday evenings, do you know?" asked Holmes.

She frowned, and then smiled. "I do not frequent the King's Arms myself, you understand, but I can make enquiries of one who does. Our gardener, Tompkins, would be able to answer that question better than I can myself."

"There is no need to put yourself to any trouble," said Holmes. "Mine host will be able to oblige with that information, I am sure. Thank you for your time, Miss Scythorpe. You have been most helpful," he continued, picking up his hat. "May I trouble you in the future, should I require more information?"

"You are always welcome to visit, Mr. Holmes. I lead a quiet life, and your visits will provide me with some relief from the monotony in the life of a poor vicar's daughter."

As we made our way from the Vicarage to the inn, my eye was caught by a man of somewhat villainous aspect. It was clear that Nature had not favoured him with a handsome face at birth, but the additions of the distorted cauliflower ears of a pugilist and a deep scar creasing his cheek from brow to chin, combined with a ferocious scowl, gave him one of the more hideous countenances I had met in my life. Though we had been warned that Mathews, if it were he, did not respond to greetings, I nonetheless hailed him with as cheery a "good morning" as I could achieve, but it was ignored as if I had not opened my mouth.

"The unsociable George Mathews, we may assume," remarked Holmes, when we could assume ourselves to be out of earshot. "He has certainly lived up to his reputation."

Over lunch at the inn, Holmes made discreet enquiries concerning Mathews, and received the information that he was a regular customer there. On being asked as to whether

Mathews appeared in the public bar on Friday evenings, the landlord scratched his head.

"That's funny, now you come to mention it, sir," he replied. "I don't remember seeing him of a Friday, though many of the other servants from the Big House come here those nights. Mark you, it's a busy night for us, is Friday, but it's not a face you'd miss in a crowd, if you'll pardon my saying so, sir."

Naturally I was intrigued as to why Holmes had asked that question, but held my peace as we made our way through an excellent steak pie.

"And now," said Holmes, "let us pay a visit to the icehouse where our late friends are supposedly at rest."

I was horrified by this proposal. "Do you believe that Mr. Soames or his family will give you permission to enter?" I asked.

"I anticipate no such welcome," Holmes answered with a smile. "I do not propose to trouble the household over such a trivial matter."

"But you do not even know where to start looking," I objected.

"That, my dear Watson, is not the case. As we passed the park on our way from the station, I noted a mound with a door leading into it which can only be the icehouse. And as luck would have it, there is a stand of trees between the entrance and the house. There is a way for us to enter the park, and from there, into the icehouse, without being seen from the house."

I had serious misgivings as to the wisdom of this course of action, but knew from experience that it was useless to deflect Sherlock Holmes from a course of action once his mind had been made up on the subject, as was obviously the case here.

Accordingly, not twenty minutes after the above conversation had taken place, we found ourselves standing in front of the great wooden door of the icehouse – a typical example of its type, being a thick stone-walled construction covered with sod, into which ice was placed in the winter, and packed with straw, where it would keep cool and unmelted throughout the warmer months of the year.

Though the door was locked, this did not serve as a deterrent to Sherlock Holmes, whose skill at picking locks would have been the envy of many a criminal. With a satisfying sound, the lock opened, and we stepped through the portal into the cool darkness of the icehouse.

" Close the door, Watson," Holmes commanded me. He struck a match, and by its light I saw the switch of an electrical lighting apparatus, which he engaged, flooding the place with a glare that hurt my eyes. As I became accustomed to the bright light, I saw two plain deal coffins, resting in the middle of the pile of ice blocks.

Holmes moved towards these, and motioned to me to join him. The lids of the coffins had been removed, revealing their occupants, whose heads lolled at an unnatural angle on their shoulders, the necks having been broken by the hangman's rope.

My friend bent forward and examined the corpses. " Grafton and Kimble," he murmured to himself. He might almost have been reciting a prayer. " Two of the very best at their work in their time, and two of the very worst of characters." Suddenly he stood up with an exclamation. " Halloa! Watson, take a look at their left hands."

I looked, and with a start of horror drew back. The left hand of each man had been severed at the wrist. At Holmes' request, I bent forward and tried to determine by what method the hands had been removed.

" I would have to say they were removed using an axe, but not a particularly heavy or sharp one," I concluded. " At least two blows have been struck in each case, where a heavy sharp axe could have accomplished the deed in one stroke."

"An axe such as this?" suggested Holmes, a small hatchet in his hand. "I would imagine that this is provided for the purpose of splitting the blocks of ice, but judging by the stains on the head, I deduce that it has been used for these foul deeds." He pulled out his ever-present lens and examined the axe closely. "Yes, as I thought," he said.

"But for what purpose would anyone do such a thing?"

"There is something that I have read someplace about an ancient custom or superstition, but discarded as being of no relevance in today's modern and scientific age. But the whole business is so fantastical and incredible, in the truest sense of the word, as to make my knowledge irrelevant to the business at hand, if you will pardon the somewhat macabre play on words. And yet at present I can conceive of no other solution."

He examined the bodies again, and called my attention to the fact that a lock of hair had apparently been removed from the scalp of each man. It was I, however, who noted the earthenware pot, filled with a coarse grey powder, with what appeared to be blue fingernails protruding from it.

"I believe the powder to be salt," said Holmes, when I had called his attention to this curious collection, "and I am confident that if we were to dig in it, we would discover both left hands."

"Does all this add to your surmise?" I asked him.

"I believe that it does," he said, sadly. "Come, let us away. I have seen what I did not expect to find, but it is enough, anyway."

We turned out the electrical lighting, and opened the door a crack to ensure that we would remain unseen, before slipping outside, where Holmes used his picklocks to reseal the entrance.

As we passed the small copse that stood between us and the house, I called Holmes' attention to the trap, with Mathews on the box, drawing up outside the front door. Thanking me for the notice, he silently withdrew a small pair of opera-glasses from his pocket, and proceeded to observe the three figures emerging from the front door of the house, who entered the trap,which then set off down the drive.

"The Misses Devereux, and their mother, if I am not mistaken," he observed. He passed the glasses to me, and I discerned our visitor of the other day, together with another young woman who could only be her sister, if facial resemblance was to be my guide, and an older woman. This last was dressed in the height of fashion, in a style which, to my eyes, was more suited to a young woman of her daughters' age than to a mature matron. I remarked as much to Holmes, and with a faint smile, he repeated a saying about mutton and lamb, which I will not trouble myself to repeat here.

We set off on our return journey to the inn, Holmes seemingly unconcerned about the ghastly scene that we had both witnessed in the ice-house, and discoursing lightly about the joys of bee-keeping, a study for which he expressed a predilection, should he ever find time for such relaxation.

"And what," he asked me, as we sat down to a cup of very welcome tea in the parlour of the inn, "do you make of Miss Scythorpe?"

"She is no beauty," I answered him.

Holmes smiled. "I was not referring to her outward form, though you are correct to mention it, in that it may have some bearing on the case."

"She is obviously well acquainted with the Devereux family," I said.

"Very true. Very true indeed," he repeated almost dreamily. "What do you make of her mention of the missing brother?"

"He is obviously the black sheep of the family. No doubt he was packed off to Australia or some such location, after the usual trouble involving a servant girl or some such."

"It is usually the girl who is sent away in these cases," Holmes reminded me.

"Maybe he was caught cheating at cards?" I suggested.

"No doubt it is something of that type," agreed Holmes. "And what of Miss Scythorpe?" he asked again.

"She seemed to me to have a good head on her shoulders, as you said to her. She obviously has little regard for Soames."

"Other than for his good looks, for which the poor girl obviously envies him, having few of her own. Yes, you are right, she despises him. It is Mathews who interests me more. Why should a mere valet be taken into his master's confidence in such matters? Especially since he seems willing to allow the matter to be known for a financial consideration."

"Do you attach any importance to the fact that he is not here at the King's Arms on Friday evenings?"

"Of course. We know he is no foe of the demon alcohol, and yet he spends his Friday nights away from the place where he most reasonably might be expected to be. You do not consider that to be strange?"

"Maybe he uses another inn?" I suggested, but even to my ear, my words sounded a little unconvincing.

"At any event, I will attempt to engage him in conversation, should he enter this inn."

We enjoyed a hearty dinner, and settled down in the private bar of the inn, from which it was possible to keep an eye on the comings and goings in the public bar. At about eight o'clock, Sherlock Holmes sat up. "He has just entered," he announced. "Will you join me in a pint of beer in the public bar?"

I had to admire Holmes' insouciance as he strolled into the public bar, seemingly oblivious of the effect that he produced among the workmen and labourers drinking there. He made his way to Mathews, who was awaiting his turn to be served, and clapped his hand on the man's shoulder. "I know you, don't I? You took on the Tipton Smasher and knocked him out inside the second round with a perfect right cross. You fought under the name of the Ludlow Lad, as I recall." Holmes' voice had taken on accents other than his usual, reminding me a little of a West Country man.

Mathews looked startled and not a little suspicious. "How do you come to know all that? You follow the Fancy, do you?"

Holmes laughed easily. "I saw you fight in London once, didn't I? I never forget a man who makes me money, and the money I laid on you that day returned to me many times over. I am, as you have so astutely observed, a student of the Fancy. Allow me to repay you. Three glasses of your finest, landlord," he called out.

He received the drinks, and Mathews took a table with us in the corner.

"Your health, sir," said Mathews, raising his glass, "and yours, sir," to me. "Now, what can I be doing for you?"

"Why, nothing," said Holmes airily. "I was simply repaying the favour that you did for me."

"That was ten years or more back, begging your pardon. No-one remembers that sort of favour for that long. Now stop your codding and tell me what you want done for you."

Holmes appeared to be embarrassed. "It's a matter of a woman... " he began hesitantly.

"Ain't it always?" the other roared with laughter. "They're nothing but trouble, Mr. ...? "

"Smith," replied Holmes blandly. "And my friend and associate, Mr. Jones," indicating me.

The other's eyes gleamed with a roguish smile. "Very well, Mr. 'Smith'," he replied, with an emphasis that showed that our aliases held little credibility in his eyes. "How do you think I can help you?"

"I wrote some letters which I now regret having written," Holmes told him. "The woman in question, to whom I wrote them, still holds them, and refuses to return them to me."

"Unless you pay up?" asked Mathews brusquely. Holmes nodded. "Blackmail, eh? You want the letters back? Can't say I blame you there. We've all done things in our time that we're sorry for later, haven't we? How much does she want for them?"

"Two thousand pounds," replied Holmes, quietly.

Mathews let out a low whistle, and his jaw dropped. "That's a lot of money, Mr. 'Smith'. They must be some letters, to be worth that much to you."

"As you have guessed, I have not given you my real name," said Holmes. "There would be complications in the nation's politics, were the mere existence of these letters to become public knowledge, let alone their contents."

"And you want them back?" Again Holmes nodded. "Why do you think I'm the one who can get them back?"

"Maybe not you personally, Mr. Mathews, but I was under the impression that you might have friends who were in a position to assist me. In your days as the Ludlow Lad, you were acquainted with a certain Bill Lewis, were you not?"

The other's face turned pale, and he stared at Holmes. "Now how in the name of ____ would you know that?"

"It is my business to know such things," replied Holmes, calmly.

"Bill's dead, you know. He wore the broad arrow for seven years in Dartmoor, and it broke him, it did. He came out and died within the six months."

"Dear me, I am sorry to hear that," said Holmes calmly. "But I am sure you have other friends in the same profession? Friends who possess a certain skill in acquiring objects from others' houses?"

"D___ you, Mr. 'Smith'! What if I do?"

"Sit down and listen to me." Holmes laid a calming hand on the other's sleeve, and spoke in a voice of command. "I am prepared to offer a large sum of money to the man who brings me those letters."

"Not two thousand?"

"Of course I am not prepared to pay two thousand. Seven hundred."

"Twelve hundred."

The bargaining went on for a few minutes, and eventually closed at one thousand pounds.

"Where are they?" asked Mathews.

"In London. If you give me your address, I will send you the details by letter. You can read, I take it?"

"Of course I can read, but I'd sooner not have letters coming to me where I am right now, if you don't mind. If you can address them to a lady I know who lives here in the town, that will do me well." To my astonishment, he then proceeded to give the name and address of Miss Scythorpe. I am sure that my consternation was visible, but since Mathews was not looking in my direction, it went unnoticed by him. For his part, Holmes appeared to show no surprise at this knowledge, but gravely inscribed the name in his notebook.

"Very well, Mr. Mathews. You may expect a letter from me within the week, which will contain the details of our little business, and the methods by which you may contact me."

"And the money?" asked Mathews, truculently.

"Cash on delivery, my dear fellow," replied Holmes, with a nonchalant air. "But if you insist on something in advance—"

"I b_____ well do," retorted the other.

"Here are ten pounds on account," Holmes told him, opening his pocket-book and handing over two banknotes.

Mathews grumbled, but accepted the money, after receiving Holmes' promise that more would be forthcoming with the letter that would arrive the next week.

"A pleasure to have made your acquaintance, Mr. Mathews,"

said Holmes, swallowing the last of his beer. "Come, Jones," turning to me, "we must make our way to the station if we are to catch the train to Town."

I obediently followed Holmes out of the inn, and started walking in the direction of the station.

"I am assuming that you do not wish Mathews to know that we are staying at the inn, and thereby discovering our identities from the landlord," I ventured.

"Precisely, Watson. You are coming on nicely. I fear we will have to take the train in the direction of Town. Mathews is following us. He is not as stealthy in his movements as he believes he is." He chuckled in the darkness.

At the station, we bought two first-class tickets to the next station along the line to London. "Let us hope that he does not enquire our destination of the clerk," said Holmes, as we boarded the train. "I fear we will have to walk back, but it is a fine night with a good moon, and a matter of a mere five miles or so."

"With pleasure," I replied. The smoky air of the inn had given me a headache, and I was anxious to have a chance to dispel it. "What do you make of our new friend's acquaintance with Miss Scythorpe?" I asked.

"I confess I was surprised by that news. However, on reflection, I can see several possibilities connected with this."

"I see none," I retorted.

"I see none clearly," admitted Holmes, "and it would therefore be premature for me to reveal them at this stage."

We reached the station where we alighted, and commenced our walk back to the inn. Our path took us past the Vicarage, and to my surprise, despite the lateness of the hour, I beheld a shadowy figure, whom I recognised as Mathews, leaving the house by the back door.

Holmes likewise remarked the fact, and laughed in that peculiar almost noiseless fashion that I had come to know so well. " He is wasting no time," he said, " in informing his confederate of the arrangements that he and I have made."

" Are you not concerned that she will inform him of our true identities ? " I asked.

" You make a fair point," admitted Holmes, " but I do not consider that she will do so. Why should she associate a Mr. Smith who is returning to London tonight with Sherlock Holmes, who is staying at the King's Arms ? "

I saw the justice of this remark, and refrained from further comment on the matter.

The next morning, Holmes announced that we were going to pay a call on Soames. " You need not fear that Mathews will see us and recognise his companions of last night," he told me, anticipating and forestalling my objections. " I am sending a message by one of the village urchins, informing him that his presence is urgently required in the next town. I am confident, by the way, that Soames will be at home. Today is Friday, and we were told that he has almost invariably made his return from town on that day of the week." He showed me the message he had written, formed in a crude unlettered hand, and signed merely with a " J", inviting Mathews to discuss " a mater of grate importans" at the inn in the next town.

" It could be from James or John," said I.

" Or Jack or Jonathan or Joshua," added Holmes with a smile. " Yes, I am sure that he will be able to put two and two together and thereby make three."

At that moment, the boy to whom Holmes had referred earlier entered the room, and Holmes presented the letter to him, with strict instructions not to reveal anything to Mathews regarding the identity of the sender. We watched through the window as the lad hurried out of sight, and made his way to the house. " I expect him to pass this way on his path to the station in under thirty minutes' time," said Holmes, and applied himself to his pipe.

As prophesied, Mathews passed the window within twenty minutes of the lad's departure, hurrying towards the station, and swathed in a heavy muffler that partly covered his face.

"Now!" said Holmes, and we set off from the house.

The maid who answered the door and to whom we gave our cards informed us that Mr. Soames was indeed at home and would be happy to see us. We were ushered into a large room that appeared to be a library. Our host had obviously arisen from his armchair to greet us. He was a man of moderate height, and as we had been told, was of more than usual handsomeness. It was easy to imagine a lonely widow falling for his glossy black hair, flashing dark eyes, and trim moustaches, combined with a face that spoke of intelligence and sensitivity.

His voice, however, gave somewhat of the lie to his appearance, being in some indefinable way not that of a gentleman, and corresponding to no dialect or accent with which I was familiar. His words were civil enough, though, as he greeted us, made us welcome, and enquired pleasantly about our visit.

"As a business associate, and dare I say it, a friend of the late Mr. Devereux," Holmes told him in answer to his question, "I felt it was my duty to pay a visit on the household."

"Quite, quite," murmured Soames. "Your name is Sherlock Holmes, I see. Any connection to the detective?"

"That is myself," replied Holmes, and I fancied I saw a look of fear come into the other's eyes at these words.

"May I enquire the nature of the business you conducted with Mr. Devereux?" asked Soames, and there was a distinct touch of nervousness in his speech.

"I fear that I am not at liberty to disclose the private matters which have been entrusted to me by my clients," said Holmes in an even tone, "even when the client may be deceased. I am sure you understand."

"Of course," said Soames, but his attitude from then on became considerably more guarded.

Holmes made small talk with him for a few minutes, and it soon became obvious that whatever qualities Soames might possess, a quick mind was not among them.

"Are you gentlemen staying long?" he asked. "I have company this evening, but I would be delighted to invite you to luncheon tomorrow." His tone, however, was not expressive of delight.

"Alas," Holmes sighed. "We must return to London in a matter of less than an hour, but perhaps we may accept your hospitality at some time in the future."

"Oh, any time, any time," said Soames, with a marked lack of enthusiasm in his voice.

We made our farewells, Holmes asking to be remembered to Mrs. Devereux, and "Gerald, Eliza, and Mary". The name of Gerald produced a frown on Soames' face, but he said nothing as he acknowledged Holmes' request.

"Are we really returning to London?" I asked, as we made our way down the drive towards the town.

"To be sure we are. If we catch the 11:13 and change for the express at Rugby, we should arrive in London well before Somerset House closes."

"You wish to see the death certificate for John Devereux, the father?"

"I have no reason to suspect anything related to that death. No, I wish to see if there is a death certificate for Gerald Devereux. You remember what Miss Scythorpe told us? No? She started to talk about his death, and then suddenly corrected herself and talked about a disappearance. Obviously she was attempting to conceal the fact of the brother's death from us for some reason."

"And you wish to find out when and how he died?"

"Indeed. The certificate, should I be able to locate it, will at least direct me in the nature of any further enquiries."

The journey back to London was spent in near silence, but

as we passed Watford, Holmes suddenly spoke.

"Did you remark anything about Soames?"

"Other than his looks and the fact that he obviously is lacking in intelligence and education, very little."

"You failed to observe, for example, that he has obviously earned his trade as a groom and a coachman in the past?"

"Indeed I did. On what do you base that assumption?"

"It is not an assumption, my dear Watson, it is a deduction based on scientific evidence," he replied a trifle testily. "Surely the particular malformation of the left hand caused by the frequent holding of the reins of a carriage would have informed you of his profession, even if you had failed to note his peculiar stance, typical of those who work with horses. Added to which, the 'Pink 'Un' thrust down the side of the armchair in a vain attempt to hide it from our view should have told you the class of person with whom we were dealing."

I accepted Holmes' words on the matter, though in truth I had failed to note any of the points that he mentioned.

We arrived in London, and Holmes immediately hailed a cab to take him to Somerset House.

"Shall I come with you?" I asked him.

"No, no, you may return to Baker-street. Meet me here at Euston Station at five-thirty. If you can talk Mrs. Hudson into providing us with a picnic dinner to refresh ourselves on the journey, so much the better."

"We are returning tonight?" I asked incredulously.

"Indeed we are. I am sure that our departure for London will have been communicated in some way to Soames and Mathews, who will therefore find this Friday to be uninterrupted, and a convenient time for the regular meeting with the roughnecks about whom we were informed by Miss Devereux. Staying at the same inn as these men, we will be in an excellent position to observe and make further plans. Half-past six here," he reminded me, climbing into the cab. "Do not fail to be here."

I followed Holmes' instructions, and was waiting at Euston Station at the appointed time. Mrs. Hudson had risen to the occasion, and I was equipped with a small hamper containing an excellent cold repast.

" Well done, Watson," Holmes remarked to me, and remarking the hamper as we boarded the first-class carriage. " I see your afternoon as been as profitably spent as my own."

" You discovered something of interest, then ? "

" Indeed I did," rubbing his hands together. " Young Gerald Devereux died some two years ago, in the town to which we are now travelling. The idea of his being sent away was a false trail."

" And the cause of death ? "

" It was given as ' drowning'. Intriguing, no ? "

" Indeed so."

" I have the name of the doctor who signed the death certificate. It is more than likely that he is still in practice, or at least living in the town. He will be our first port of call tomorrow."

" And tonight ? "

" We observe. Now let us perform another investigation," he said, opening the hamper. " Excellent, Watson. Mrs. Hudson has done us proud."

On arrival at our destination, Holmes and I deposited our scanty luggage at the inn, and we made our stealthy way to the Devereux house, where we lay in wait by the icehouse in a position where it was possible to watch all comings and goings.

We had not long to wait before two roughly dressed men appeared, walking down the drive towards the house. Holmes produced a pair of opera glasses from inside his coat, and studied the couple. He whistled softly. " By George ! " he exclaimed in an excited whisper. " I fancy that our friends at the Yard will be glad to see this pair of beauties safely locked away. Though I have always considered that they have their base here in the Midlands, I know that they have been active in London, but have lacked the evidence to ensure their arrest and conviction."

"You know them, obviously?" I asked.

"Indeed I do. I see before me James Dowell and Earnest Haddon, two men at the top of their profession, which is housebreaking. I have little doubt that they have been summoned here at least in part as a result of our conversation last night."

To my surprise, it was Soames, and not Mathews, who opened the door to these men.

"I had expected that," said Holmes. As we watched, the lights went on in the room that I judged to be the library where we had held our conversation with Soames, signifying, to my mind, that some sort of conference was being held there.

"Shall we listen at the window?" I said to Holmes, but he shook his head.

"No, I fear that we would not hear anything, and the risk of discovery while it is still light is too great. Maybe after sunset, in about an hour's time, I guess."

In the event, we were surprised by the emergence of Soames from the house, making his way to the stable block.

"Surely they cannot be leaving already?" Holmes muttered to himself. "It is not yet dark."

We waited, and soon a horse drawing an open dogcart appeared from the stables, with Soames driving it.

"I had assumed that the purpose of a carriage after dark was to protect the identities of the visitors," mused my friend. "It would appear that this is some other purpose."

Soames dismounted from the box, and appeared to re-enter the house by a door that was invisible to us. Within two or three minutes, another door opened, and four men : the two visitors, Mathews, and Soames, left the building and started to walk in our direction.

"Fool that I am!" Holmes whispered. "I should have guessed that this would be their destination. Quick, Watson, there is no time to lose!" Somewhat inelegantly, we hurriedly moved behind a bush, hoping that our movements would not be noticed by the approaching group of men.

To our relief, they did not appear to have noticed us, and made straight for the icehouse door. It was now possible to see that the two housebreakers, Dowell and Haddon, were carrying lengths of sacking. Mathews inserted the key in the lock, the door swung open, and the party entered the icehouse. The electrical lighting inside was activated, and light streamed in the dusk from the chinks surrounding the now reclosed door.

We waited, not daring to move, and our patience was rewarded after about ten minutes, when the four men emerged, carrying two long sackcloth-swathed bundles, one to each two men. Mathews and his partner put down theirs as the lighting was extinguished and Mathews closed and locked the icehouse door, and the pair resumed their burden, following the other two and walking towards the dogcart, where the bundles were deposited. It did not take the skills of Sherlock Holmes for me to deduce the contents of the sacking.

Soames remounted the box, and the two visitors sprang into the cart, whereupon Soames whipped the horse into a slow walk, and the cart set off down the drive. Mathews re-entered the house, and shut the door.

"Shall we follow?" I asked Holmes.

"No," he replied, shaking his head. "I fear it would profit us little to do so."

"But what is the meaning of all this?" I asked.

"I have a strong suspicion that it is as foul a business as I have ever encountered," said Sherlock Holmes, "and I do not say that lightly. I can hardly believe that I would ever encounter such a thing in this modern scientific age." He paused in thought for a moment, and then spoke. "Come, I believe there will be little more to see here tonight. Let us return to the inn."

On our return, Holmes, by means of decoying the landlord on an errand for some hot water to be carried to our room, managed to catch sight of the entries in the hotel register for the two visitors. "As I thought, Watson," he explained to me, "they have not bothered to register under the names that their mothers gave them. They both have given an address in a town in Staffordshire, though, and though the addresses are undoubtedly false, the town itself may well be their place of residence. It may be as well to telegraph to the police of that town early tomorrow morning and advise them that these two rogues will be returning by train."

"And we will be visiting the doctor tomorrow?"

"Indeed so." He stretched mightily and yawned. "It has been a hard day. I will smoke a last pipe before turning in."

On my waking the next morning, I discovered Holmes had already arisen, and had walked to the post office, where he had somehow arranged for the telegram to be sent to the provincial police before the post-office had opened. "We will not take breakfast until our two friends have departed the inn," he announced, entering the room as I was shaving. "I have just dispatched a wire to the Staffordshire Constabulary informing them of the existence of these villains who will soon be returning, and advising them to search their lodgings for evidence of the proceeds of the robbery at the Duke of Northampton's London house the other day."

Eventually, we made our way downstairs and broke our fast most satisfactorily with eggs and home-cured bacon. "And now for the doctor," said Holmes, wiping his thin lips with the napkin, and rising from the table.

On enquiry, the residence of Doctor Hawthorne proved to be close by, and a matter of a few minutes' walk brought us to a handsome villa set in a carefully tended garden. The door was opened by an elderly woman, who introduced herself as the doctor's housekeeper, and led us to the study, where Hawthorne received us.

He was an elderly man, somewhat stooped, but his white hair framed a face that bespoke a considerable alertness and intelligence.

Upon our introducing ourselves, he smiled. "I have heard of you, Mr. Holmes," he said. "I have spent many happy hours reading of your adventures as recorded by Doctor Watson here, and I am happy to make your acquaintance. I trust that you are not here on any business connected with your line of work?"

"As it happens, I am engaged on a case where your help would be invaluable," Holmes told him.

A look of surprise came into the other's face. "Dear me! I had no idea that I would ever figure in one of your mysteries," he said. "Do you suspect me of a crime, or one of my acquaintances, perhaps?"

"My dear doctor," Holmes answered him, laughing, "I merely wish you to furnish me with some information which will fill the gaps in my knowledge."

"I will do my best to assist you."

"I believe that it was you who signed the death certificate of Gerald Devereux, who met his end by drowning two years ago."

A cloud passed over the old man's face. "Yes, it was I who signed the certificate. Why do you ask? Is there any doubt concerning the cause of death? I assure you that I am as certain of the diagnosis as any that I have made in my life."

"No doubt exists in my mind," said Holmes. "However, I was hoping that you might be able to provide me with some more details concerning the circumstances of the death."

"I will do my best," replied the other. "Gerald was a

cheerful youngster–I had known him since he was a young child, and I was a friend of his father, whom you may also know passed away following a hunting accident some three years ago. I had the unhappy distinction of certifying the deaths of both the father and the son, a circumstance which gives me no pleasure, believe me." He stopped, and wiped his eyes with his handkerchief. "Forgive me, but at one time I would have counted the Devereux family as my own, but since Mrs. Devereux' remarriage—" He broke off. "At any rate, Gerald was, as I say, a bright and cheery lad, but a cloud seemed to fall over him after his father's death."

"That is hardly unnatural," I remarked.

"I agree, but the cloud was of an uncommon nature. It did not appear to be the grief that is usually occasioned by the loss of a parent, but seemed to stem from some other cause. Indeed, though Gerald seemed to exhibit a perfectly natural filial grief, there was some deeper shadow that passed over him about a year after his father's death. This is not unknown in adolescents, of course, particularly under such trying circumstances, but in the case of Gerald, it was of such intensity that I became fearful for his safety. In the event, my worst fears were realised."

"Why? What can you mean?" I asked, though I believed that I already knew the answer to my questions.

"I mean that Gerald Devereux killed himself by drowning. His body was found fully dressed at the bottom of the pool at the deepest part of the river, with the pockets of his jacket and trousers filled with stones. I have no doubt whatsoever in my mind that it was his intention to kill himself. The body was seen, and I was called immediately, before the body was even retrieved from the water. I was able to remove the stones from the pockets without attracting attention, and accordingly, I could certify the death as an accident, rather than as a suicide. I am aware that I may have acted against the law, but I believe that it was all for the best." He paused, and once again dabbed at his eyes.

"It may be an offence," admitted Holmes, "but I hardly think that it is a serious one, and I am sure that should the facts of the matter ever come to light, you will be exonerated for what you have just told us. Can you make any guess as to why this black mood should have come across this young man's life?"

"I can do more than guess," the other sighed. "However, I feel that it is not for me to divulge the secrets of another, even when that other has passed from this life."

"You are sure you cannot do more?" asked Holmes.

"I fear that I cannot, in all conscience. If you really do desire further knowledge of this matter, I would suggest that you contact Miss Lydia Scythorpe, though I warn you that the subject is a delicate one, and she may be reluctant to discuss it with you."

If Sherlock Holmes was surprised by this speech, he hid it well. "We have already spoken to her," he told Hawthorne, "but not regarding this subject."

At that moment, the heavy slow tolling of a church bell sounded from outside the window. "What might that be?" I asked the doctor.

"Ah, that will be for the funeral," he replied, shaking his head sadly.

"What funeral is that?" asked Holmes.

"The funeral for the two friends of the husband of Mrs. Devereux, as I still think of her. That is to say, Mr. Soames."

"What do you know of them?"

"Only what is common knowledge around the town. That is to say, that they are London friends of Mr. Soames who died indigent, and to whom he wished to give a decent burial here in this town. The bodies were brought from London some days ago, I believe, though no-one saw them arrive."

"And the local undertaker has been responsible for all arrangements?" asked Holmes.

"I cannot say, but the story I have heard is that the bodies were already in their coffins when they arrived in the town, and have been stored in the icehouse in the park since their arrival."

"I see," said Holmes. "I take it you will not be attending these rites?"

"I have no love for Soames," the old man told us firmly. "I dislike speaking ill of others, but I must tell you in confidence that he, in my eyes at least, is far from being a gentleman. I have to confess that I consider that Martha Devereux made a grave mistake in marrying him."

"We called on him yesterday," Holmes told him. "I lack your extended acquaintance with him, but I fear that my views concur with yours as regards his being a gentleman. Lacking any knowledge of Mrs. Devereux, I cannot speak to that matter."

"Is there anything else with which I can assist you?" Hawthorne asked.

"At present, no, but I may wish to ask you some more questions in the future, if I may."

We were shown out, and I started for the inn, but Holmes gripped my sleeve. "Wait!" he said. He turned towards the church, where a small cortège, consisting of Soames and a woman dressed in black, were following two coffins, borne by pallbearers, towards a couple of open graves. "Watch them carefully," he said, as the coffins were lowered into the ground. "Those are not empty, judging by the way they are being handled."

"And yet I would swear that we saw their contents removed last night."

"Indeed so. Yet another mystery. Come, let us return to the inn, and thence to London," he said, as the earth showered down on the coffins.

At the inn, we were greeted by the landlord, who presented Holmes with a telegram. " Came for you just now, sir," he said.

Once we were in our room, Holmes ripped open the envelope. " Excellent ! " he cried. " This is from the Staffordshire Constabulary, and thanks me for the information I passed to them. Dowell and Haddon were taken as soon as they stepped off the train, their lodgings were searched, and the bulk of the loot stolen in the Northampton robbery was discovered there. I am pleased to have withdrawn these two from circulation, at least temporarily, until they can face the Assizes. Of course, they may turn Queen's Evidence, but I have my doubts there."

We arrived at Euston Station, and Holmes hailed a cab to take us to Cavendish-square.

" Not Baker-street ? " I asked.

" On this occasion, I wish to see the Home Secretary."

I could hardly refrain from laughing. " Do you think that the Home Secretary will wish to see you at home, even supposing that he is in London over the week-end ? "

" I believe so," he told me seriously. " Her Majesty's Government surely owes me a few small courtesies. I shall be seriously annoyed if he has failed to honour the request in my telegram that I sent to him this morning when I sent the other to the Staffordshire police."

" And your reason for wishing the Home Secretary to remain in London on a summer Saturday ? "

" Surely that is obvious. I wish him to sign an exhumation order for those two coffins we have just seen buried."

" You expected this ? "

" Perhaps I did not expect the burial to take place today, but I certainly expected it soon, and I wished to be prepared."

I looked at Holmes with respect. I could not conceive of

any other man who would have considered and prepared for an eventuality such as this.

We arrived at the house of the Home Secretary, and Holmes sent in his card. We were admitted immediately, and the statesman greeted Holmes familiarly.

"I would not put up with this sort of thing from anyone else, you realise, Holmes. Indeed, if it were not for your brother, Mycroft…" He let his voice trail off.

"It is very good of you to spare the time, sir," replied Sherlock Holmes, in as humble a voice as I had ever heard him employ.

"Nonsense, Holmes. I know enough of you and your methods to know that you would not waste my time on trivialities." He picked up a piece of paper. "Now what are the names on the graves for which you wish the exhumation order?"

"I am unsure of the exact names on the graves, sir, but the names of those supposedly in them are Thomas Grafton and Francis Kimble."

"Those two, eh? They gave us enough trouble when they were alive, and they continue to do the same after their death. Very well, I am sure you have your reasons." He took a pen and wrote the names in the appropriate place on the paper, and signed it with a flourish. "There you are, Holmes. I trust that this is worth my stay in London."

"Once again, I apologise, sir."

"By the way," called the Home Secretary, as we turned to leave. "I would remind you that tomorrow is a Sunday, Holmes."

"Sir?"

"I think that the local vicar may well have an objection to an exhumation carried out on a Sunday. I know that you prefer to work fast, but a little decorum in these matters may ensure better cooperation, eh?"

"Of course, sir. Thank you for the reminder."

Once outside the front door, Sherlock Holmes began to laugh. "I suppose that he has a valid point regarding its being a Sunday tomorrow. Given that fact, I suggest that we, too, regard it as a day of rest. We must ensure, though, that Mathews is out of the way before we start the digging. I think it is necessary for Mr. Smith to invite him up to London to discuss the retrieval of those letters that we discussed earlier. Come, to Baker-street, and then for a touch of the exotic at an excellent little French restaurant that was recommended to me by a man whose judgement in such matters is to be trusted. What say you?"

I readily agreed, and on our arrival at Mrs. Hudson's, Holmes composed and dispatched his reply-paid telegram to Warwickshire. We enjoyed our meal in Soho, and discovered a reply when we came back.

"Very good," said Holmes. "I will meet and deal with Mathews here in London on Monday. I have arranged to meet him in the waiting-room at Charing-cross station at 11 in the morning. You, Watson, will take this," handing the exhumation order to me, "up to Warwickshire tomorrow night, and arrange with the police that it be carried out some time after nine the next morning, when Mathews may be assumed to be on his way to London."

"And Soames?" I asked.

Holmes waved his hand negligently. "Soames is of little importance in this matter. You may, however, ask the police to arrest him once the exhumation has been performed."

"On what charge?"

"Whatever seems best to the police," was the reply. "Whatever seems most appropriate for a grave-robber and falsifier of official documents."

"You are sure that you do not want to perform all this yourself?" I asked.

"I would not have asked you if that were the case," he

answered me with a little asperity. “ It is a perfectly simple matter, and you can handle it with ease.”

“ Very well,” I replied.

As requested, the Sunday evening saw me taking the well-remembered route from Euston, and I visited the police-station as Holmes had requested.

The name of Sherlock Holmes appeared to mean little to the sergeant on duty behind the desk, but the inspector to whom he referred me was all smiles as he came to meet me, his hand extended.

“ Doctor Watson, indeed, a pleasure,” he said to me. “ Is Mr. Holmes not with you ? ”

“ I fear not,” I replied, “ but I bring a message and a request from him.” I briefly explained Holmes’ request, and set the exhumation order in front of him.

“ These burials were only carried out on Saturday, were they not ? ” said the good Inspector Jeavons, a look of puzzlement creasing his honest face.

“ Indeed so,” I answered him, and went to to explain how Holmes had recognised and arranged for the arrest of the two men who had visited the Devereux house on Friday. I said nothing of the icehouse and what we had seen there. “ There is a very good reason to believe that these men are intimately connected with the exhumation.”

After a little further discussion, the officer was convinced of the necessity of the operation and the need to perform it the next morning, and agreed to provide the men and make the necessary arrangements.

“ Very good, Doctor. After nine o’clock, you say ? And you are staying at the King’s Arms ? I will make sure that my men call upon you before that hour.”

I took myself to the inn, where the landlord welcomed me as an old friend. “ Your friend isn’t with you ? ” he asked.

“ No, I am alone,” I answered him. “ Why ? ”

"The lady at the vicarage left this for him," he said, and handed me an envelope, inscribed in a female hand, "For the Attention of Mr. Sherlock Holmes".

"I will make sure it reaches him," I said, and took the envelope up to my room.

Following an early breakfast the next morning, I was visited by a police sergeant and a constable, bringing some concern to the landlord of the inn, who was obviously under the impression that I was about to be arrested. I calmed his fears, and went with them to the churchyard, where Inspector Jeavons was waiting with two sextons equipped with spades.

"Which one first, sir?" asked one of the workmen.

"I think it is immaterial," I said. "This one," pointing to the nearest, which happened to be that of Francis Kimble.

The two men set to work. The soil was still loose, and it was a simple matter for them to reach the coffin. "Shall we open it down here, sir?" one of them called from the pit in which they now found themselves.

"Yes," shouted down the inspector.

The two set to work with their tools, and soon removed the lid to reveal a coffin that was empty other than for a mass of sodden straw.

"What's all this?" asked Jeavons. "You men were among the pallbearers on Saturday, were you not? Surely you can tell the difference between an empty and a full coffin?"

"Begging your pardon, sir," one replied, "but the coffin we buried here on Saturday was full."

"Well, get on with the other one," exclaimed the police officer impatiently, and turned to me. "What do you make of this, then, Doctor?"

"Let us wait until the second coffin has been opened before I make a pronouncement," I said, "but I have a pretty shrewd idea what has been happening here."

After a short time, it became clear that the second coffin

was in the same state as the first; that is to say it was empty, save for some wet straw. "A funny thing here, sir," called up the workman. "I've never seen holes like this in the bottom of a coffin." He moved the straw aside, and we could see a pattern of holes, each about half an inch in diameter, which had been bored into the base.

"What was buried here, then?" the inspector asked me, having received assurances from the workmen that the coffins had indeed appeared to be full when they were buried.

"Ice packed with straw," I told him. "The ice has melted, and the water has run off through the holes in the base of the coffin."

"Of course, it seems elementary now that you mention it," said Jeavons. "But it leaves an unanswered question. Where are the bodies?"

"I can tell you something about that," I said, "but I would sooner tell you back at the station, in privacy."

"Very good. I will require you as a witness to my statement in any case. Very good, men," he called to the workmen. "I suggest you remove the coffins from the graves and leave the graves open. Inform the vicar of what has happened, and then I want you at the station to put your names to the statement that I will prepare."

We set off for the police station, and once there, I recounted the macabre events that Holmes and I had witnessed a few nights previously. At the end of my recitation, the inspector called in the sergeant who had brought me from the hotel. "Take two or three constables with you, go to the Devereux house, and bring in Soames and his man Mathews," he ordered. "Also, you will enter the icehouse. If you see a bucket containing salt and… other things, then bring that here. Resist the temptation to look inside the salt to see what is there."

"If all is well, Mathews will be in London, dealing with

Sherlock Holmes," I informed them.

"Am I to arrest them, sir? If so, on what charge?"

"No, I simply want them here to answer some questions. And if Mathews is indeed in London, bring Soames alone."

"Very good, sir."

The sergeant left, and the inspector leaned back in his chair and looked at me. "You seem to be a clever man, Doctor. What is your impression of what is happening?"

"I am as puzzled as are you," I admitted. "I can make little sense of this. Why would these men take the bodies of two executed criminals, remove their hands, and then keep the hands in salt?"

As we were puzzling over this conundrum, a constable knocked on the door.

"Excuse me, sir, but the Reverend Scythorpe wishes to see you," he said.

"This will be a complaint about our digging in the churchyard, no doubt," Jeavons said to me. "Perhaps you would be good enough to explain the whole situation regarding the Home Secretary to him, Doctor."

But when the Reverend Scythorpe entered the room, it was obvious that he had more on his mind than excavations in his graveyard. His face was pale and haggard, and he entered the room wringing his hands.

"My daughter, Lydia," he positively wailed as he came in. "You must find her!"

"She is missing, then," said Jeavons. "When did you notice she was gone?"

"She did not appear at the breakfast-table this morning. There is nothing unduly alarming about that. Sometimes she sleeps late, and I have not the heart to insist that she rise at a regular hour for breakfast. But it is now past eleven o'clock, and at half-past ten she had not appeared. I went to her room and knocked on her door, but there was no answer. The door was unlocked, so I went in, but it was clear that her bed had not been slept in the previous night."

"I see," said the inspector, who had been making notes as the distraught father told us his story. "When did you see her last?"

"Yesterday afternoon," said Scythorpe. "I had a meeting of the parish council, and then I took Evensong, and when I returned home, I assumed that she had gone to bed. I did not see her at the service in church, but sadly, that is not an unusual occurrence. I am now reluctantly accustomed to her absences from Divine Service."

"Have you any idea where she might be found?"

The other spread his hands wide in a gesture of despair. "None, none. I confess that since her mother died some years back, Lydia has been self-willed and has gone her own way. I am unable to form any definite opinion of where she might be now."

"Well, of course we will do everything in our power to find your daughter, Mr. Scythorpe, but she is an adult and responsible for her own actions. I am sure that no harm has come to her, but rest assured that we will do what we can. Come!" he called, as there was another knock, and the sergeant who had been dispatched earlier appeared in the doorway.

"Mr. Soames is ready to see you, sir," he told us. "There was no bucket such as you describe in the icehouse."

"Soames, eh?" said the vicar. "I am not one to speak ill of others, but..." his voice trailed off. "I suppose I must leave you, but I do trust, Inspector, that you will do what you can to find my Lydia. She is my only child, you know."

The vicar left us, and Jeavons instructed the sergeant to inform all the constables on duty of the missing girl. "Almost certainly, she will turn up safe and sound," he said to me, "but we should put the Vicar's mind at rest."

When this had been done, Soames was sent in. He started

when he saw me. "I was under the impression that the police wanted to talk to me," he said, somewhat truculently. "What is this man doing here?"

"He is working with the police," said the inspector in a firm tone that brooked no argument. "Anything you can say before me you can say before him. Now, what has happened to the bodies of the two men who were supposed to be buried in the churchyard on Saturday? It's no use your trying to deny the matter. We have received and acted on an exhumation order signed by the Home Secretary himself, and opened the graves. We know that you packed the coffins with ice and straw." He leaned forward, and spoke in a menacing tone. "Where are those bodies?"

"You'll never find them," said Soames in a weak voice. "They'll have gone by now."

"What do you mean by that?"

"I will tell you no more," said Soames. "I am under no obligation to do so. I am a free man, am I not?"

"At present you are," said the police officer. "And at that, you are more fortunate than your friends Dowell and Haddon, who are now under arrest in the cells in Tamworth police station." Soames looked shaken. "How…? What…?" he stammered.

"And the items that they stole from the Duke of Northampton's London house are safely recovered," I added.

Soames' face had turned a deathly white. "You've no evidence that I had anything to do with that," he exclaimed, and then suddenly fell silent.

"Why, Mr. Soames," said Jeavons pleasantly. "Why on earth would you ever believe that you would ever be suspected of such a thing? A fine upstanding citizen like you?" His voice positively dripped irony, which was not lost on Soames. "Perhaps you would prefer us to arrest you, so that you can clear your name in court?"

"Yes, or rather, no. I don't know what I mean," wailed Soames. "None of this is my doing. It's all Mathews' work, I tell you."

"Perhaps you would care to dictate a statement?" suggested the inspector. "I think it may go some way to persuading the judge to giving you a lighter sentence when you are sent for trial. You are not under arrest, but I think it is my duty to warn you that anything you say may be used in evidence against you. You will remain here at the station."

"I should never have listened to her," Soames sobbed. "It has all been a ghastly mistake."

"Take him out and sit him at a table in the room next door to wait for me," Jeavons told the constable standing outside the door.

The inspector and I looked at each other. "Did he mean Mrs. Devereux just now?" asked the inspector.

"I have no idea who was meant," I answered him.

"Telegram for Doctor Watson," interrupted one of the constables, holding out an envelope to me.

"It is from Holmes," I announced when I had read it. "ARREST SOAMES IMMEDIATELY STOP WILL ARRIVE BY SPECIAL TRAIN STOP MATHEWS ARRESTED STOP HOLMES END"

"On what charge does he say we should arrest Soames?" asked the inspector.

I shrugged. "He does not say. Let us wait for his arrival, and we will hear all. I am sure you can detain Soames until then. The telegram was dispatched less than an hour ago. We may expect him soon."

In the event, it was less than two hours before Sherlock Holmes strode into the police station. I was somewhat shocked by his appearance, however. A cut lip and a bruised cheekbone formed striking additions to his appearance.

"How did you come by those?" I asked, taken aback.

"All in good time. The coffins were empty, of course?" I

nodded. " Where is Soames ? "

" In that room," said Jeavons, pointing to a closed door.

" Excellent. He is under arrest ? "

" On what charge was I supposed to arrest him ? " asked the policeman.

" Why, as an accessory before and after the fact of the robbery at the Duke of Northampton's London house, of course. Had you not made that elementary deduction, Watson ? " Ignoring my protests, he went on, " It would also seem wise to question Miss Lydia Scythorpe regarding her part in this affair."

" I think, sir," said Inspector Jeavons heavily, " that you owe us some explanations. As to Miss Scythorpe, she has gone missing since at least yesterday evening, so your suggestion that we question her is somewhat impractical at present."

I suddenly remembered the letter I had been given the previous day by the landlord at the inn, and presented it to Holmes, who tore open the envelope. He appeared to have read only a few sentences before he raised his eyes from the paper, and stared at the inspector with something as close to panic as I had ever seen him display.

" Where was Gerald Devereux' body found ? " he asked.

" By the river, in the woods. In the deep pool. Why in the name of the Devil are you asking this now ? "

" Because that is where you will find the body of Miss Lydia Devereux, if I am not mistaken. Come ! " He swept out of the room, the inspector and I following helplessly in his wake. " Can you swim ? Good. Come ! Bring ropes and hooks ! " he shouted to two constables in the passageway, and they joined the party, following a nod from their superior officer.

It took us some twenty minutes to reach the spot, and on the way, I enquired further regarding Holmes' face.

" Oh, that," he chuckled. " I fear that my left canine is now a matter of history, thanks to the fists of the erstwhile Ludlow

Lad, who is now in the Bow-street cells on a charge of assault. I will tell you more anon."

We reached the fatal spot and we could easily see that Holmes' prediction had been fulfilled. A still form, clad in white fabric, lay at the bottom of the pool, the only movement being the cloth rippling in the current of the river.

Jeavons gave orders to the constables to bring the body to the surface. "How did you know—?" he asked Holmes.

"The first few sentences of this letter. Here." He retrieved the letter from his pocket and read aloud, "'My dear Mr. Holmes, By the time you read this, I will have joined my dear Gerald in that place where he left me for ever. I heard about Dowell and Haddon. I am guessing that Soames and Mathews are next, and then it would be my turn. But it shall not be. Farewell, Lydia Scythorpe.'"

"Clear enough as a suicide note," nodded the inspector. "But what is this connection with Soames and Mathews and the other two?"

"All in its place," replied Holmes. "Let us deal with one thing at a time."

The constables, with some difficulty, retrieved the body and laid it on the bank. Holmes felt around the skirts, and nodded sombrely. "Stones in the pockets. She left herself no room for second thoughts or remorse."

"The poor girl," said I, with feeling. "What could have driven her to this?"

"The shame of exposure and arrest," said Holmes. "You may feel sorry for her, Watson, but she was the ultimate moving spirit behind many of the robberies carried out throughout the country over the past year or so."

The police officer started. "Will you explain this?" he demanded, in an angry tone. "I would remind you that withholding information from the police is an offence. I think that you owe us some kind of account."

" Softly," said Holmes. " You have all you need before you, save the minor details. Let us bear Miss Scythorpe to the mortuary, and then someone must inform the vicar of the loss of his daughter."

" That is my responsibility," said Jeavons. " Mr. Holmes and Dr. Watson, please return to the station and await me there."

We did as we were bid, and Holmes completed his perusal of another handwritten sheet that had been enclosed with the letter, nodding in agreement from time to time as he read it. " No, Watson, you may read it later," he said to me. " For now, I wish to assemble the facts that I have just learned."

He sat in silence with his eyes closed, opening them only when the inspector entered the room.

" I have done this many times," said Jeavons, " and informing the relatives of the deceased is never pleasant, and never becomes easier."

" That is very true," I said, with feeling. " I have never become accustomed to the task."

" Mr. Holmes, perhaps you can now tell us of your theories."

" No theories," said Holmes mildly, " since what I had deduced has been corroborated by this sheet here which was enclosed with the letter from Miss Scythorpe. I have, however, discovered some motives which were unknown to me. Let me begin by saying that the guiding spirit in the Devereux household was not Soames, the supposed master of the house, but Mathews, the valet. Furthermore, the meeting with Mrs. Devereux which led to the marriage between her and Soames was no accident. It had been arranged by Miss Scythorpe."

" Why ? " I asked. " Why would she wish to bring about such a match ? Was she unaware of the kind of man that Soames is ? And of Mathews' past ? "

" On the contrary," my friend replied. " It was for that very reason that she contrived to being them together. I had my suspicions of this, but lacked proof of a motive until I read this letter. Lydia Scythorpe loved Gerald Devereux, and it seems, from what she has written to me, that the affection was fully returned. Unprepossessing in appearance she may have been, but it seems that at one time she must have possessed a character which was sweet and affectionate. Gerald's father approved the forthcoming match, but on his death, Mrs. Devereux, whose acquaintance I have yet to have the pleasure of making, forbade her son any further intercourse with Miss Scythorpe."

"On what grounds?" asked the inspector, who had been making notes.

"For the most trivial of reasons, Miss Scythorpe writes. On account of her looks. Mrs. Devereux, according to this letter, was concerned about the possible appearance of her future grandchildren."

"Absurd!" I burst out.

"There is another reason that occurs to me, though it is not mentioned in the letter. Mrs. Devereux may have regarded the girl as a fortune-hunter, determined to seize as much of the late John Devereux' property as possible. At any event, the mother's interdiction cast a cloud over the son, and as we know, he took his own life."

"That was an accident," protested Jeavons.

Holmes shook his head. "It was no accident. I refuse to reveal the source of my information, but I can assure you that Gerald Devereux' death was suicide. This is confirmed independently, by the way, by the mention here of a farewell note by Devereux to Scythorpe. Very well, then. The poor girl was distraught, not unnaturally, and sought revenge on the mother, while still retaining friendly relations with the girls of the family. She had done charity work among the poor in the cities, and there had come into contact with some of the lowest of the low. Among these were Mathews and Soames. Both had been in service, Mathews as an under-footman, and Soames as a coachman, but had pursued other lines of business as house-breakers, and had additionally been engaged in pilfering from their employers. So much can be learned from their police records.

"Soames has good looks of a kind, and a plausibility about him which inspired Scythorpe to set him at the widow Devereux. Once installed as her new husband, he would have control of the estate, and would in all probability bring the Devereux household into ruin and bankruptcy. Mathews, as I mentioned, was the guiding spirit of the two, and would be brought in as some sort of personal servant to Soames. I imagine the relationship provided much secret amusement to the pair.

"In addition, as the respected master of a considerable prestigious estate, Soames, or rather, his alter ego, Mathews, would be in a position to organise criminal gangs. Who would ever think of looking for the meeting place of a gang of housebreakers in such a house? We know that every Friday, Mathews invited his confederates to plan the next week's robberies, which were carried out at the start of the week, as I discovered from my researches. If these activities were discovered and made public, the shame and embarrassment attached to Mrs. Devereux' second marriage would surely preclude any good marriage by her daughters. Indeed, it is quite possible that Mrs. Devereux was well aware of the activities of her second husband and his valet, but preferred to keep silent."

"I know that many of us in the town had our doubts about Soames, but this ..." exclaimed Jeavons.

"I confronted Mathews with all this at Charing-cross station when I met him earlier today," continued Holmes, "revealing my true identity. His denial was swifter than I had anticipated, and came in the form of a stinging right that has cost me my left canine. For all that he retired from the Fancy some years ago, his punch is not to be ignored. However, neither is mine, and I emerged, somewhat battered, as you can see, but victorious. Mathews is now in the cells at Bow-street, but I anticipate that other charges will be added to the original one of assault very soon. I leave the exact formulation to your discretion, Inspector."

"It all seems so unbelievable," I said.

"Hell hath no fury ... " replied Holmes. "I have seldom encountered such a cold-blooded, calculating scheme, designed to bring a whole family to ruin. There is another aspect that you may care to investigate at more length, Inspector, and that is the possibility that Miss Scythorpe was being blackmailed by this pretty pair. She certainly blackened their names enough when she spoke to us about them, did she not, Watson? I believe that when she talked to us, she was in some hopes that their activities would be curtailed, but when the time came for their arrests, her nerve failed her, and she decided that the music would remain unfaced by her."

"But there is one thing you have left unexplained," said the inspector. "The bodies and the empty coffins."

"This is a macabre and grisly business," said Holmes. "Has either of you ever heard of the Hand of Glory?"

Both Jeavons and I shook our heads.

"Accounts vary as to the exact nature of this superstition," said Holmes, "but it was popularly believed by members of the criminal classes in the past that a candle made of the fat rendered from the corpse of a hanged man, and held in the preserved left hand of that corpse would either render the holder invisible, or else render all in the house immobile, save him who held the Hand of Glory. You can see how a robber would value such an article, should it actually exist."

I shuddered. "Grisly indeed. I think it is easy to see the pattern now that you have explained the superstition."

"One of the members of this gang obviously still believed

in this tale. Soames, or rather Mathews, arranged with the authorities that the corpses of two executed criminals be given to him for burial, claiming some humanitarian motive. He claimed that they were friends of his," said Holmes. "It may well be the truth, in that they had a past acquaintanceship. Once the bodies had been placed in the icehouse, the left hands were removed."

"As I told you, Inspector," I interjected.

"The bodies were presumably removed on Friday night to a place where the fat from the bodies could be removed and candles created from it." Holmes ignored the looks of disgust from both Jeavons and myself and continued. "Of course, something had to be provided for the burials, and the coffins could not be empty. I assume that they were filled with ice packed in straw."

"Indeed, that is what was used."

"The hands would be pickled according to a recipe involving salt and various bodily fluids. There are also various so-called magical ceremonies to be carried out before the Hands of Glory can be used. I am sure that Soames will tell you all about it, Inspector, should you wish to know the details. My friend Tobias Gregson at Scotland Yard has charge of Mathews, by the way, when you need him here."

"Well, Mr. Holmes, it would appear that you have wrapped this up pretty neatly," said Inspector Jeavons. "You will, of course, be available to give evidence and to appear at the inquest of Miss Scythorpe?"

"If you feel it is really necessary," said Holmes. "However, I have a commission on hand from one of the Royal Houses of Europe which may require a protracted absence from the country. But you may always address correspondence to me at 221B Baker-street. Come, Watson. We must away."

Once in the train, I could not forbear from asking Holmes how he reached his conclusions.

"When we saw the corpses in the icehouse with their left hands removed and in the bucket of salt, it immediately put me in mind of the Hand of Glory, an old story which had somehow stuck in my mind since the time I read about it as a student. Of course, the legend of the Hand of Glory was believed only by criminals, and since the master of the house was involved, he must thereby be of that class. 'Like master, like man,' we were told by Lydia Scythorpe, and that set me to ask myself which was the master, and which the man. The rest was a matter of elementary research in the police-court records. It helped, of course, that I had some personal knowledge of Mathews' past, but otherwise, this was a trivial case, with little of interest to it, save the deliberate forcing of the nuptial hand as a method of revenge. That is, to my knowledge, unique in the annals of crime."

And so Sherlock Holmes lightly dismissed a case which I confess still sends a chill down my back as I relive those days.

The Adventure of the Disappearing Spoon

F all the cases associated with my friend, the celebrated consulting detective Mr. Sherlock Holmes, one of the most amusing was this, which I have chosen to entitle "The Adventure of the Disappearing Spoon". There are those who may feel that the events related here are too trivial to have engaged the attention of the man I consider to have possessed the greatest mind of his age, let alone be worth the setting down in print, but I nonetheless present them as an example of the kind of problem on which Holmes occasionally found himself engaged.

In this instance, our customary leisurely breakfast was interrupted by the entry of Mrs. Hudson, announcing the arrival of "a client, Mr. Holmes. He sent in his card, and said to me that you would remember him."

"Indeed I do," Holmes remarked, examining the square of pasteboard. "Arthur Bourne-Hunter. I remember him clearly from our time at school together. He was in a slightly more advanced class than I, and was a keen cricketer, as I recall, a pastime in which I took, and continue to take, little interest. Show him in, Mrs. Hudson. And another cup for his coffee would, I believe, be welcome."

Mr. Bourne-Hunter proved to be a man of moderate middle age, attired as a man of business, and a fine gleaming top hat set off the ensemble whose foundation was provided by a costly overcoat. There appeared to be a certain roughness about the collar and cuffs of his shirt, and I noticed a little scuffing around the worn heels of his boots, however.

"Well, Holmes," were his first words to my friend. "I will wager that you never expected to see me as one of your customers."

"I am always delighted to see my old school fellows," answered Holmes, "no matter to what depths they may have fallen."

The other's face fell as he pondered the implications of the words, and then he burst out laughing. "It is nothing of that nature, Holmes," he explained. "I stand accused of no crime or wrongdoing. Indeed, the matter regarding which I have come to consult you is of so trifling a nature that I would hardly consider it worthy of your attention."

"Tell me of it, all the same," my friend instructed him. "Since you appear to have followed my career with some attention, you will need no introduction to my friend and colleague, Dr. John Watson, who has been good enough to reproduce some of my cases, albeit in a regrettably sensational and dramatic manner."

I bowed towards our visitor, and he returned the salute.

"I observe," continued Holmes, "that your happy marriage has been blessed by the addition of a daughter to your family. A second child, but I condole with you on the loss of the other infant."

"It would appear that you have been keeping your eyes on my fortunes," replied our visitor, visibly astonished.

"By no means," answered Holmes. "I merely observed the charms attached to your watch-chain, the second of which is rimmed in jet, of the type which is usually worn by those who enjoy a matrimonial state and who have suffered a sad loss to their family. When I see a doll, of the type enjoyed by younger children, protruding from the parcel bearing the name of the famous West End toyshop, I conclude that your child is a girl."

"I see that you have retained the habits of your youth. Holmes here," turning to me in explanation, "was forever playing this sort of trick on us at school. And then, as now, he was always perfectly correct. But to business."

"To business," Holmes agreed.

"As I said, the whole affair is so laughably trivial that I feel embarrassed about mentioning it at all. You should know that I serve on a number of committees of organisations that do good work in a number of fields–the preservation of ancient buildings, provision of goods and lodging to the needy, and so on. The meetings of these committees are typically held at the house of one of the members, usually one of the officers. I take my turn in the hosting of these meetings, at which refreshments in the form of tea or coffee, with sandwiches and cake and so on are typically served. I am sure you are familiar with such events, Holmes?"

"By repute only," smiled Sherlock Holmes. "I move in rather different circles than do you, I fear. Pray continue your narrative."

"We are, I suppose, well-to-do, my wife and I, and we possess plate of various kinds, including a set of antique teaspoons, six in number. We keep these pieces of Georgian silverware in a case, and after one of these meetings two days ago, my wife was informed by our maid, Anne, that one of the spoons was missing. A thorough search of the kitchen, the butler's pantry, and the room in which the meeting had been held failed to discover the missing utensil. I trust my servants absolutely–they have all been with me for years, and there is no doubt in my mind that they are telling the truth when they say that the spoon is not in their possession. I regret to say that my current suspicion is that one of our guests, that is to say, one of the committee members, had abstracted it. Here is a list of those present on that day." He handed Holmes a sheet of paper torn from a notebook.

"Do you suspect any one of them in particular?"

"If you were to ask me such a question, I would have to say that each one of them is above suspicion. Four of the members of the committee meeting on that day are known to me personally, and have been for a number of years. Of those four, three are in Holy Orders in the Established Church. One is a Rural Dean, and the other two are rectors or vicars of prosperous parishes. The fourth is a Conservative Member of Parliament, Sir Augustus Derringford, tipped, so I am informed, for a place in a future Cabinet."

"And the other members of the committee that met that day?"

"I met these two for the first time on that occasion. One is a highly regarded manufacturer of patent medicines, and the other is a peer of the realm."

"I would hardly regard a peerage as a guarantee of honesty," Holmes remarked sardonically.

"Lord Fardindale is a well-known member of Society, and in his seventy-five years of life, his honesty, insofar as I am able to ascertain, has never been called into question. It is in the case of Mr. Edward Loughton that I have my doubts. He candidly admitted to an interest in old silver at the meeting and openly admired many of the pieces on display in the room where the meeting was held."

"It is he whom you suspect, then?"

"I fear so. I have made enquiries, as discreetly as is possible for me under the circumstances, but there has never been any suspicion that his fine collection of silver plate has been obtained by any means other than the usual legal methods–that is to say through purchases from dealers and at auctions and so on."

"And your wish is to discover the purloiner of this spoon, and to bring the malefactor to justice?"

"No, no, Holmes. Were this to be made public, the reputation of all the members of the committee would suffer by association. This must be done as quietly and unobtrusively as possible, without bringing the Society into disrepute. I have no doubt that you are able to accomplish this, given the accounts that Dr. Watson here has provided of your methods of working."

"Very well, I will attempt the case. By the by, can you provide a detailed description of the missing piece of silverware?"

"I can do better than that. Here is another one of the set of six spoons." He withdrew a chamois leather roll from his breast pocket, and unwrapped it to reveal a small silver spoon.

"May I retain this?" asked Holmes.

"I had a premonition that you would make that request. If you will sign this receipt, my mind will be eased, however." Holmes signed the paper, and our client made his farewells.

When we were alone, Holmes laughed in the mirthless way that was so characteristic of his moods. "He has not changed, Watson. Did you notice one thing about the conversation just now?"

"No mention was made of your fee?"

"Precisely. He was always reluctant to spend money as a schoolboy, and it appears that nothing has changed. You remarked the soles of his boots, for example? Or perhaps you failed to observe the collars and cuffs of his shirt?"

"He would appear to be generous enough to his poor little surviving child," I defended him.

"Maybe that is so," Holmes grudgingly admitted, "but it seems plain to me that he still has long pockets and short arms, as our friends north of the Border would put it."

"Your first port of call will be this Mr. Edward Loughton?"

"It is indeed the obvious place to start, but in cases like this, it may well pay me to distrust the obvious. I think that we shall begin our investigations with the Rural Dean mentioned here. We may well learn more from his description of Mr. Loughton than would be possible from an interview with the man himself. Come, let us to Dulwich."

On arrival at the house of the Reverend Frederick Bastable, we were ushered into a well-fitted room, on two sides of which stood display cabinets filled with what appeared to my eyes to be a priceless display of antique silver objects, some of them seemingly from the days of Good Queen Bess, or even before that time.

"It would seem strange for a man who is already in possession of this quantity of silver to purloin a single spoon," I remarked.

"Strange, but by no means unknown," Holmes commented. "The collecting passion is a strange one."

As he finished speaking, our host entered–a tall thin man of strangely ascetic appearance, who greeted Holmes and myself with some warmth.

Without further ado, Holmes launched into a tale of how he, as a collector of silver objets, wished to make the acquaintance of other collectors, and that the good clergyman's name had been provided to him by Edward Laughton.

"Ah, Laughton," answered the other. "I know him well. Indeed, we serve on the same committee together in a charity dedicated to good works among the poor and destitute. A most estimable man, to be sure, if inclined to impulsive action from time to time."

I have previously mentioned that Sherlock Holmes displayed an extraordinary depth of knowledge on an equally extraordinary range of subjects, and so it was here, where he rattled on about scroll feet, fluted rims, and other minutiæ of which I was completely ignorant. At length this baffling conversation came to an end and we were let out of the house.

I could not refrain from asking Holmes from where he had acquired the stock of knowledge which he had just displayed, and he gave his answer as follows.

"One never knows, my dear Watson, just when knowledge will turn out to have its uses. I retain in the lumber-room of my brain the details of many such branches of learning, in the expectation that they will at some time, as on the present occasion, fill a need."

"And your view of the good Laughton?"

"Let us determine, shall we, what exactly was meant by the description given to us, that of 'impulsive'."

Within the hour we were seated in the drawing-room of Mr. Edward Laughton, who had professed himself to be a great fan of my friend's work, and indeed, displayed some powers of observation of his own, correctly deducing that I had sat on the right side of the hansom that had delivered us to his door, based on the mud splashes on the side of my trousers.

" 'Pon my word, Mr. Laughton," exclaimed Holmes, chuckling, " if you continue in this fashion, I will have to seek other employment."

" Hardly that," answered the other. " I fear that my general build and appearance tell against me in that regard."

Indeed, Mr. Laughton was of a corpulent build, and it was hard for me to imagine him pursuing malefactors through the streets of London in the same fashion as did my friend.

" Well," laughed Sherlock Holmes, " perhaps I am safe for the present as regards competition in my profession. May I ask you about the charity committee meeting that you attended at the house of Mr. Bourne-Hunter some two days ago ? "

" I will tell you. It was not what one would term an event that was filled with excitement. Indeed, the principal interest for me was provided by the presence of some fine Queen Anne rat-tailed spoons provided for us to stir our tea. I am something of an amateur in that line, do you see, and these struck me as being particularly fine examples of their type. One thing struck me as being somewhat strange, and that was that there were only five spoons of that type provided for us, though such spoons were commonly sold in sets of half a dozen. One must have become lost at an earlier date. A pity. A complete set would be much more valuable from the collector's point of view."

" A pity indeed," agreed Holmes. " And there was nothing that struck you as untoward about the gathering ? "

The other hesitated, and appeared reluctant to speak. " I hardly like to speak against a man of the cloth, especially one as highly placed and well regarded as the Reverend Bastable, but…" His voice trailed off, and we waited in silence for a little before he resumed his speech. "It seemed to me that the reverend gentleman appeared to be a little too interested, perhaps, in the spoons I have just mentioned. But maybe it is my fancy. Were I a covetous man, Mr. Holmes, I would covet those spoons, but it is not a vice to which I consider myself to be subject."

"That is most interesting," replied my friend. "I thank you for your hospitality, and I am extremely grateful for the information. As you are no doubt aware, even the smallest of clues can help unravel a puzzle. I am not at liberty to inform you of the nature of the puzzle at present, but hope to be able to do so in a short while. A very good day to you, sir."

With that, we took our leave, but had hardly started walking down the street, when the front door of the house we had just quitted burst open, with Laughton fairly bounding out, calling Holmes' name, and brandishing a square of paper.

We turned back to meet him, as he ran to us as fast as his constitution would permit.

"This dropped from your pocket as you were leaving!" he told Holmes, handing my friend the paper, which transpired to be a Bank of England five-pound note. "I could not let you depart without it."

Holmes received the money with equanimity, but gravely thanked our erstwhile host, folding the money into his pocket-book and replacing it with care before bidding a second farewell.

"And that, Watson, has taken care of that little matter," he remarked as we hailed a cab. "Just one more trial, and we are done."

On arrival at Baker-street, Holmes immediately subjected the spoon to some chemical tests at his bench, which appeared to satisfy him as to the results.

"I think I may now safely pay a visit to Mr. Bourne-Hunter," he informed me. "Do you wish to accompany me?"

"I am astounded that you feel the need to ask me that question," I retorted. "Of course I will be with you."

"Good old Watson," he laughed. "This promises to be amusing."

On arrival at our destination, Holmes explained to Bourne-Hunter that he did not believe that any of the committee members had purloined the missing item.

"In which case, where is it?" asked the other, irascibly.

"Maybe we can discover the answer by cleaning the spoon you were kind enough to lend me. It has acquired a little tarnish. Maybe your butler would be good enough to guide us to the pantry where the silver is cleaned."

"As it happens, with the more valuable pieces, such as these spoons, I myself take responsibility for their care. I will take you to the aluminium bowl that I use for this. A bath of salt and baking soda in the bowl removes tarnish without subjecting the pieces to excessive rubbing, which can damage the more delicate items."

In a room obviously dedicated to such purposes stood the aforementioned bowl, into which Bourne-Hunter placed the spoon. "Since it is not excessively tarnished," he informed us, "a few minutes should suffice for its cleaning."

At the end of that time, he plunged his hand into the mixture, and gave a cry of surprise.

"There are two spoons in here!" he exclaimed.

"I had rather fancied there would be," remarked Holmes.

"You mean to tell me that the missing spoon was here all the time and that I have been thinking ill of..." His voice sank to a whisper. "Dear me. What a miserable sinner I am to think so ill of my fellow man. How can I ever come to terms with myself?"

"That, my dear fellow, is none of my concern. My task was

to locate the spoon. All other matters are a matter between you and your conscience."

As we sat in our rooms in Baker-street, I asked Holmes how he had come to the correct conclusion regarding the location of the missing object.

"Though I do not a priori reject a man of the cloth as a potential offender in such matters, I saw nothing in the manner or behaviour of the Reverend Bastable that would cause me to place him under suspicion. A man who displays his purchased collection as openly as does he would surely not hide the fruits of less legal acquisitions. And Laughton impressed me both by the power of his observation, as you saw, and his honesty in returning the banknote that I dropped on his floor as we were leaving. From this, I was reasonably sure that only five spoons had been presented for use. Since a thorough search of the house had revealed no trace of the missing spoon, I was forced to conclude that it had been mislaid in the journey from the case to the table. And where better than when it was being cleaned prior to its public appearance?"

"I assume that the chemical tests that you made on your sample spoon informed you of the method used for its cleaning?"

"Indeed they did. And when I discovered that no servant was employed for the purpose, but that the cleaning was performed by an enthusiastic, but incompetent, amateur, the links in the chain were complete."

"A triumph en petit, I would say," I laughed.

"Maybe, maybe," he agreed. "But it is well to remember that the same techniques may be used to track down either a missing spoon, or a murderer. The same principles apply to each. And now I suggest that we take our supper, where cutlery will play a different role."

ACKNOWLEDGMENTS

HERLOCK Holmes continues to fascinate many, long after his “ death”. I am delighted that so many people have expressed their satisfaction with my attempts to tell of his adventures, and I thank all of you who have encouraged me with your kind words, comments, and reviews.

I am also grateful to my wife Yoshiko, who has patiently endured my mental journeys to 19th-century London, and furthermore, has joined me on a more physical journey, moving our life halfway across the world, from Japan to the United Kingdom.

Special thanks are due to Jo, the late “ Boss Bean” of Inknbeans Press, who supported me and helped me create more and better than I would ever manage unaided.

Also by Hugh Ashton

Sherlock Holmes Titles

Tales from the Deed Box of John H. Watson M.D.

More from the Deed Box of John H. Watson M.D.

Secrets from the Deed Box of John H. Watson M.D.

The Case of the Trepoff Murder

The Darlington Substitution

Notes from the Dispatch-Box of John H. Watson M.D.

Further Notes from the Dispatch-Box of John H. Watson M.D.

The Death of Cardinal Tosca

Without My Boswell

1894

Some Singular Cases of Mr.Sherlock Holmes

The Adventure of Vanaprastha

General titles

Tales of Old Japanese

The Untime

The Untime Revisited

Balance of Powers

Leo's Luck

Beneath Gray Skies

Red Wheels Turning

At the Sharpe End

Angels Unawares

The Persian Dagger (with M.Lowe)

Titles for Children

(with Andy Boerger)

Sherlock Ferret and the Missing Necklace

Sherlock Ferret and the Multiplying Masterpieces

Sherlock Ferret and the Poisoned Pond

Sherlock Ferret and the Phantom Photographer

The Adventures of Sherlock Ferret

About the Author

Hugh Ashton was born in the United Kingdom, and moved to Japan in 1988, where he lived until a return to the UK in 2016.

He is best known for his Sherlock Holmes stories, which have been hailed as some of the most authentic pastiches on the market, and have received favourable reviews from Sherlockians and non-Sherlockians alike.

He currently divides his time between the historic cities of Lichfield, and Kamakura, a little to the south of Yokohama, with his wife, Yoshiko.

He may be contacted at hashton@mac.com.

If you enjoyed this book...

HANK you for reading these stories – I hope you enjoyed them.

It would be highly appreciated if you left a review or rating online somewhere.

You may also enjoy some of my other books, which are available from the usual outlets.

CPSIA information can be obtained
at www.ICGtesting.com
Printed in the USA
FFHW011321090919
54880347-60574FF